Can you love too much?

"I'm worried about you, Lacey," Kit said. "You've got to promise me you'll stay out of these wild stunts."

I felt like a rubber band being pulled in two directions at once. I wanted to promise Kit anything. Yet the thought of Megan all alone—

"Please, Kit. Try to understand."

He shook his head, his face clouded with anger and frustration. "Promise me you'll stay away from her."

The band pulled tighter. I couldn't breathe. How do you choose between the two people you love most in the world?

Dear Reader,

Thanks for picking up this Changes romance. We hope that you'll enjoy reading it as much as we've enjoyed bringing it to you.

Our goal is to present realistic stories about girls in true-to-life circumstances, with relationships and problems that readers will understand and appreciate. In other words, we want to try to capture the changes you're probably facing in your own life today.

We hope we've succeeded, but the only way we can know for sure is to hear from you. Please write us or your favorite Changes authors, and tell us what you liked (or didn't like!) about the Changes romances you've read. Tell us how we stack up against your other favorite books. Tell us about the kinds of stories you'd like to read in future Changes novels: What does romance mean to you? What kinds of characters do you identify with? Where should the stories take place? What sort of problems or conflicts should a Changes heroine encounter? In this way, we can bring you more of the stories *you* want to read.

Again, thanks for reading this Changes romance. Our address is printed below. We hope you'll look for the new Changes romance each month, and we hope to hear from you very soon.

Sincerely,

Chloë Nichols

Chloë Nichols
Editor
Daniel Weiss Associates, Inc.
33 West 17th Street
New York, N.Y. 10011

A *Changes* ROMANCE

LOOKING OUT FOR LACEY

CHERYL ZACH

HarperPaperbacks
A Division of HarperCollinsPublishers

HarperPaperbacks *A Division of* HarperCollins*Publishers*
10 East 53rd Street, New York, N.Y. 10022

Produced by Daniel Weiss Associates, Inc.
33 West 17th Street, New York, New York 10011.

First printing: April, 1992

Printed in the United States of America

HarperPaperbacks and colophon are trademarks of HarperCollins*Publishers*

10 9 8 7 6 5 4 3 2 1

For my daughter
Michelle Nicole Wasden,
who, like Lacey, is a
special and caring person,
with much love.

CHAPTER

ONE

When the rock hit my window, I knew it had to be Megan.

I had been sleeping soundly, dreaming of Kit. Opening my eyes reluctantly, I stared at the clock on my bedside table: twenty past one. I wanted to close my eyes and try to recapture the last wisp of my dream, leaving Megan to extract herself from whatever mess she was in. But in a moment I heard the sharp twang of another rock hitting glass. Groaning, I thrust back the covers.

Pushing up the heavy old-fashioned window sash, I peered into the chill darkness. I could just make out Megan, pale beneath the winter-bare plum tree.

At least I didn't see any blood. The last time she woke me in the middle of the night, Megan had flipped over Bobby Jenkins's Jeep and been tossed twenty feet on a gravel road.

"Lacey! About time you woke up."

"What's wrong?" I tried not to speak too loudly. Thank goodness my parents slept at the other end of the house.

"Mrs. Frog locked me out again. Come down and let me in."

"Go back across the street and ring the bell till you wake her." I still regretted my interrupted dream. Mrs. Frogmorton was the latest in a long line of housekeepers who, for most of Megan's seventeen years, had been the only ones who tried to control her; they had invariably failed.

"I can't. She turns off her hearing aid when she goes to bed. Lacey, hurry up. I'm freezing!"

I could see her shivering. Sighing, I closed the window and felt for my robe and slippers. Tiptoeing—my dad wouldn't wake if the roof fell in, but my mother slept lightly, and I didn't want another argument about Megan—I made it down the carpeted stairs and ran to unlock the back door.

"Took you long enough," was Megan's only thanks. She headed for the refrigerator without waiting for a reply. "I'm starving; what's there to eat?"

I glared at her back, but admonitions were worse than useless with Megan; they only spurred her on to more reckless feats the next time. She reached for the handle, and I thought her hand seemed a little unsteady.

"Megan! Have you been drinking? You promised me—"

"Relax, mother hen." She bent to inspect the interior of the fridge. "I went to the Quick Mart, but there's a new clerk, and he wouldn't sell us any beer without an ID. So we drove to Thanville, but the stores were closed by the time we got there."

"Drove—with whom?" I knew she didn't have her father's station wagon. His big Cadillac he used for traveling; the station wagon was for the housekeeper's use.

3

After Mrs. Frogmorton had tried a half dozen hiding places, all of which Megan discovered, the woman had taken to wearing the car keys on a chain around her neck. Megan hadn't figured out how to beat that system yet.

"Jay-Jay took me on his bike. Only thing, I didn't have a jacket, and the wind cut right through me." She still shivered, despite her thick sweater. Mississippi winters harbor a particularly damp and bone-chilling cold.

I thought of the massive motorcycle and shivered myself. Jay-Jay had broken three bones in his last spill and still carried scars on his face. But I could picture Megan on the back of the bike—her long, shapely legs clinging to the heavy machine, blond hair flying in the cold wind.

"I thought Jeannie was Jay-Jay's girl."

"So? I don't want to keep him; I just wanted a ride." Megan pulled out some leftovers and began to munch on a chicken leg, ignoring my frown.

Megan made me think of one of those Greek gods of war, always leaving a trail of havoc behind her. None of the boys could resist her. I spent a lot of time while I was growing up wishing I could look like Megan, with her delicate face and long pale hair.

Me, I'm just good old Lacey, sensible and so-so in looks, with brown hair and brown eyes—not deep blue eyes that lifted a little at the corners, like Megan's, so that she always looked as if she hid a private smile.

Then I remembered what day it was. "Megan! When I brought you your gift this morning and invited you over, you were sure your dad would be home tonight."

She turned, chewing on the chicken, and didn't meet my eye. "He called, said he got held up."

So, now I knew why Megan had been careening around the countryside behind a high-school dropout. I felt a little sick.

It was Christmas Eve, Christmas Day now. I had spent the evening with my parents. Kit came over for a couple of hours, even though his married sister and her family were visiting at his house, and we had a few minutes alone in front of the fire. While Dad helped Mother finish the pies for Christmas dinner, we held hands and talked. I had had all that, and Megan had waited alone for her only parent, who hadn't come.

So when Megan dumped the chicken bone into the garbage, I followed her toward the stairs, burdened by the odd guilt that a person with great wealth feels before someone impoverished.

At the door I said, "Megan—your boots!"

It wasn't just that they were coated with mud; they would make too much noise on the stairs.

I thought she was going to protest, but even Megan didn't want to face my mother at two in the morning. She stooped and tugged off the high-heeled boots, leaving them in the corner, and we tiptoed upstairs.

Once safely in my bedroom, I eased the door shut, then pushed the pile of stuffed animals off the other twin bed.

"Want a nightgown?"

The air was chilly, and Megan nodded. "What'd you get for Christmas?"

We always opened our family gifts on Christmas Eve. Megan knew the routine.

"The cashmere sweater I wanted. Electric curlers. More clothes." It wouldn't compare to whatever extravagant gifts her dad would bring whenever he showed up. That used to bother me a lot, too.

"And look—Kit brought me this." I showed her the small velvet jeweler's box, and Megan's eyes widened. Then, when I flipped open the lid, she said, "Oh, a locket. That's nice."

I looked down at the small gold locket, not wanting to admit that I had felt the same tiny disappointment when I opened the box, thinking that it might have held— well, something else. But the locket was lovely.

"Look," I said, opening the minute catch. Inside there was an engraving that read, "To Lacey, from Kit."

"Nice." Megan sounded bored.

I held the small gold heart for a moment, savoring the inscription. All that was missing was one four-letter word. I knew Kit cared about me, but he couldn't seem to say it.

"I'm surprised you didn't wear it to bed." Megan's tone was edged with sarcasm, and I winced.

"I would have," I confessed, "but I was

afraid I might break the chain; it's very fragile."

"Why didn't he get a heavier one? Too cheap?"

"Megan!" I picked up a hapless stuffed bear and slung it at her. Caught by surprise, she yelped and threw it back at me, following the bear with a long-eared dog and a rag doll I'd had since I was two.

The doll, frail with age, split at a seam. Gray stuffing flew up into my face, making me sneeze.

"Megan," I hissed. "How could you?" Outraged, I cradled my abused baby for a moment, then jumped for Megan.

She went down under my pummeling, even though she's taller and more agile. For a few moments I pounded her on her back and shoulders, solid blows that released my anger and resentment. Then, when I realized that she had stopped fighting and hid her face beneath her hands, I drew back.

"Megan, are you okay?"

"Sure." Her voice sounded husky, and I tried to see her face. I hadn't seen Megan cry since she was six, when she fell off the garage roof and broke her ankle, and I broke my collarbone falling after her, trying to pull her back.

We'd been through a lot, Megan and I. Sometimes I felt that I'd spent my whole life looking out for Megan—a pretty thankless task, mostly. But I knew why it was always me who ended up pulling her out of scrapes—she had no one else.

Anger gone, I felt absurdly guilty. "You shouldn't have said that. Kit works hard for his money; he's saving for college, and he has to help his mother."

"I know, I know. He's a saint." She sounded tired instead of sarcastic, so I just shook my head.

"So why do you say those things?"

"I guess I wish I had someone, too," she whispered.

I could hardly hear her words, but I understood. Megan, who could have any boy in town, almost, still had no one special. No one like Kit.

"Sometimes it hurts too much," she murmured so low that I could barely hear. "There's so much emptiness inside me."

So I hugged her—my best friend from across the street—as if we were five years old again. That was the year we decided to be sisters. We swore an oath of eternal loyalty under the big azalea bush in my front yard. I brought tea cakes and lemonade, and Megan made up wonderful stories. Megan made everything brighter and more exciting.

We'd definitely been through a lot together.

She slipped out of my grasp quickly—being held made Megan nervous—but she whispered, "Lacey?"

"Yes?"

"It was a stupid thing to say." Which was as close to an apology as Megan would come.

"That's okay. Merry Christmas."

"You too. Happy New Year and all that stuff."

Forgetting our quarrel, I thought of my locket and the reflection of firelight in Kit's hair. "It's going to be a great year," I murmured. Which only goes to show how wrong you can be.

CHAPTER

TWO

When I woke, the other bed was empty. Not made—Megan wasn't strong on ordinary courtesy—just empty. I got up, made both beds—if Megan had gotten out of the house before my mother saw her, I wouldn't have to listen to another lecture—pulled on jeans and my new sweater, topped off, of course, by Kit's gold locket, and hurried downstairs.

A good smell drifted out of the kitchen. Mother bent over the stove, peering into the oven.

"The turkey in already?" I asked.

"Uh-huh. Your uncle and aunt should be here by two. Merry Christmas." She gave me a quick kiss on the cheek before turning back to the stove. She wore the new blouse Dad had given her last night.

"Can I do anything?" I asked.

"Not right now; you can set the table later. There are sausages; would you like an egg?"

I nodded, watching her quick, efficient movements around the kitchen. "Where's Dad?"

"In the shower."

I glanced at the corner, then away again. A slight deposit of dried mud revealed where Megan's boots had sat. Perhaps Mother hadn't noticed.

Dad came into the kitchen just as Mother dished up the scrambled eggs. "Good timing," I told him.

"Merry Christmas, Lacey." He gave me a kiss, then patted Mother on her rear, pulling her into a bear hug that almost upset the platter of eggs. "Merry Christmas, beautiful!"

Mother only laughed. "You're about to lose your breakfast, Romeo."

Looking smug, Dad sat down at the table. He's a good guy, my dad, if a bit old-fashioned.

I had almost finished eating when I heard a familiar knock at the door.

"I've got it," I yelled, sprinting for the front of the house.

When I opened the door, Kit stood with his shoulder against the door frame, sunlight gilding his blond hair. His grayish blue eyes glint with intelligence, and now they reflected his smile.

"How's my best girl?"

"Great—now," I said, leaning into his arms. "I thought you and your mother and little sister were leaving for Biloxi this morning?"

"We are, but I had to deliver an official Christmas kiss first."

His lips were firm against mine. When he released me, I stepped back reluctantly. "My best present yet," I told him, trying to keep the wobble out of my voice. "Except one." I touched the gold locket at my neck.

Kit grinned. "Think about me while I'm gone."

As if I had a choice. "I'll miss you," I said.

He nodded. "Me, too."

He glanced down at his watch, and I saw how long and golden his lashes were. "I have to go, Mom's waiting."

After one last squeeze, he released my hand. I could still feel the warmth of his grip.

"I love you," I whispered to his back as he walked toward the street, but he didn't hear.

One day I would say it out loud, and Kit would smile and say, "I love you, too."

The phone rang as I came back into the house. "I'll get it," I called toward the kitchen.

Megan sounded breathless with excitement.

"Lacey? Come over right now. You'll never guess what I got!"

"Five minutes," I promised, curiosity leaping inside me.

"Hurry!"

I leaned around the corner to say, "I'm going over to Megan's; she's got some fantastic gift to show me."

Mother frowned; I hoped she wouldn't start again about Megan being a bad influence. Dad shook his head. "One more extravagance to allay Stan Willowby's guilt."

Mother said, "Now, Adam. Megan's his only child. He must feel something genuine, despite—" She stopped, but I knew the rest of her thought.

"Do you think he'll ever settle down in Rockford?" I asked. Odors of cooking filled the warm kitchen. Dad sat at the table reading the paper, while Mother flipped through a cookbook: all ordinary and humdrum and very comfortable. Megan had never had this.

"I doubt it." Mother pushed a strand of brown hair back from her eyes. "He did try, the first year after his wife left. He stayed here almost three months, then said he couldn't take this backwater dump and took his old job back on the road."

Dad, who liked this "backwater dump," snorted and turned a page. But I was still thinking of Megan and her father. "Doesn't he realize how much she misses him? I mean, he's all she's got, and he's never here."

Mother shook her head. "Her aunt in Ohio wanted to adopt her, after her mother left, but Stan Willowby was too angry to allow it. I think she still writes to Megan."

I nodded. "And Megan never answers."

"Why not?" Dad asked.

"Because it's her mother's sister," I told him, taking a jacket from the peg by the door and walking across the street.

The Willowby house was directly across from ours, a white frame, like our house, but much bigger. Stan Willowby sold electronic equipment to hospitals and apparently did well, judging by the big sedan that sat in front of the house, not to mention the money he occasionally lavished upon Megan.

I knocked on the door, although I don't usually bother. Knowing that her father was home made me a little shy. No one seemed to hear, and I was about to turn the knob when the door swung open abruptly.

"Lacey!" Megan exclaimed. "This way!"

She pulled me inside and toward the back of the house. What was it—a mink coat? Not many people in Rockford, Mississippi, wear mink coats, but that wouldn't bother Megan. But we kept going through the house and out the back door. When I saw it, I gasped.

"Megan! I don't believe it."

No wonder she was so excited. A ing red convertible, neat and trim sporty, sat in the back drive.

Even from Stan Willowby this was quite a gift. I touched the scarlet paint reverently, afraid to leave a fingerprint on the smooth finish.

"Get in," Megan commanded. "I've been dying for you to come so I can try it out."

I slid into the plush bucket seat. Megan jumped in, started the engine, and pulled out of the drive with a lurch that sent me groping for my seat belt.

It was always the same. Megan, with her multitude of presents, and no one to share them with. What fun is a gift with no one to admire it? I remembered the Christmas I was six. Mother had been in the hospital again, and Dad had to play Santa all alone. With little time or money, he'd gathered a weird assortment of gifts: flannel pajamas, two incredibly ugly school dresses, a game designed for toddlers. When I went to Megan's house and viewed the pile of loot beneath her tree, I sat down and cried. Megan picked out the biggest gift—a stuffed bear with silky fur—and thrust it into my arms. That bear still sits on my bureau, and sometimes when I'm especially mad at Megan, I stroke the bear's soft fur, remembering.

The sight of a cat crossing the road pulled me out of my reverie. "Megan, look out!"

She jerked the steering wheel, and for an instant I thought we were going off the road. Then she had the car under control, and I could breathe again.

"Megan, this car won't look half as nice wrapped around some telephone pole."

Megan, still in a sunny mood, laughed and slowed down.

"Dad's going to stay home two weeks. He promised." Megan's blue eyes seemed almost luminous with happiness.

Familiar with Stan Willowby's promises, I kept my thoughts to myself. Let Megan be happy while she could.

We drove down Main Street, Rockford's one and only business center. All the small shops were closed, of course, for Christmas Day. The brick courthouse, the post office, and the branch library were deserted. No one could be seen except one old man sitting on a bench in the warm sun, and two half-grown dogs nosing through a gutter. Park benches remained one of the last visible bastions of segregation in Rockford. The diner and the coffee shop were open to all comers, nowadays. But the elderly white men sat on the right side of the courthouse, and the elderly black men on the left. Some things changed slowly, especially in Rockford.

"Looking for your bucolic boyfriend?"

I stiffened, then relaxed as I recognized the teasing in her voice. "Kit's not here; his family drove to Biloxi to visit his grandparents."

"Boring," Megan drawled. "Why didn't he stay here?"

"He couldn't." I tried not to sound defensive. "He does most of the driving for his mother. Besides, his grandfather's been ill."

A big yellow pickup truck went by, and to my relief Megan forgot about Kit.

"That's Buddy," I pointed out unnecessarily. "What's he going to say about your new car?"

"Who cares?"

Megan had gone with Buddy all the way through football season, but football had ended, and the big quarterback had apparently lost much of his appeal. Megan went through boys like a thrasher through a grain field. But Buddy had a temper, and I wondered uneasily how he was going to like being dumped.

"Let's show him what we can do." Megan put the car into gear and pulled out after the truck.

"Megan! Slow down!"

She wasn't listening. As we zoomed down the street, I prayed silently that our local sheriff was home enjoying the holiday with his family.

The pickup had turned down a residential street; Megan followed. The powerful little car passed the truck before Buddy realized her intentions. Megan beeped her horn, laughing at the expression on his face. Then, to my relief, she stepped on the brake, pulling over to the curb, where she waited for Buddy to catch up.

He pulled the truck in behind us, climbing down from the big cab. His expression was stormy as he stalked up to the car door.

"New car, huh?"

"Isn't it great?" Megan's good humor

was hard to resist; the anger on Buddy's square face began to fade. "My dad went all the way to Memphis for it."

I held my breath, hoping that Buddy wouldn't cut her down. Megan didn't get to brag about her father very often. But Buddy just nodded.

"Where were you last night?" he demanded. "I called, but all I got was the old dragon."

"What'd she say?" Megan's eyes narrowed, and I tensed. Buddy's temper was famous around school.

"Nothing that made any sense; where'd you go?"

"Oh, family stuff, you know. Christmas Eve and all that." Megan's tone was airy. I waited for Buddy to point out that Megan doesn't have any family, but he didn't.

"Well, you could have stayed home a while. If you wanted to get your Christmas present, that is."

"Really? What is it?" Megan's frown gave way to a bright smile. I could have kicked her. Had Buddy gotten a reprieve?

"Come back to the truck with me." He cast a wary glance toward me, and I felt about as welcome as a pimple on prom night. "You'll see."

Megan jumped out of the car, and they stayed inside the cab for some time; when Megan came back, she smiled broadly. Behind her, Buddy beamed like a dog who's just been patted.

"See you later," she called, then roared the red car out into the street again.

"Like it?"

I looked at her, trying to see what was new. The gleam around her neck was hard to miss.

"It's a real diamond." Megan's tone was smug.

"Very pretty." I resisted the urge to reach up and cradle my little gold locket. The locket came from Kit, and all the diamonds in the world couldn't be more precious. My faint stab of envy receded. Growing up alongside Megan hadn't been easy. But now I had Kit. Kit made me feel equal to Megan, for the first time.

As long as I had Kit . . . Even the thought of losing him left me cold. I touched the locket again, remembering the one word that wasn't there.

CHAPTER
THREE

Stan Willowby planned to leave on the first day of school. I found Megan looking bereft, her eyes unusually bright with unshed tears.

"We were supposed to go to Jackson and go shopping and have dinner, just the two of us," she muttered. "And we never did."

It seemed to me that her father had made the same promise the last time he was home. He wasn't too good at keeping promises, Stan Willowby. You'd think Megan would realize that by now, but somehow she kept on hoping.

Stan Willowby came through the front door, his briefcase in one hand, glancing at his watch.

"Hi, kid," he said. He'd only known me for seventeen years and still couldn't remember my name. Sometimes I wondered how he remembered Megan's.

"Let's hit the books, kiddo. Try to show a little ambition this time," he told Megan. "You're not totally stupid, right?" He grinned, as if this were funny.

"Sure." Megan's response held no enthusiasm.

I stared resolutely at an evergreen, but Stan didn't believe in drawn-out good-byes. He gave Megan a careless pat, then seated himself behind the wheel of the big car.

Megan ran up to the window and bent down to speak to him. "How long before you'll be home?"

"Oh, a few weeks, maybe. Depends on how tight my schedule is. I'll give you a buzz."

The big motor roared, and he pulled out with the same screeching of tires that Megan liked to affect. I stared at the bush, refusing to look at Megan's face until she finally turned and walked back to me.

"Come on," she said, her tone daring me to offer any pity.

I knew better.

"Wait till the kids at school see your car," I suggested.

"Right." Her face cleared.

She would brag to the kids at school about her father, her father and his expensive gifts. I hoped that the next bed Stan Willowby slept in had lumps, hard ones.

When we parked in the school lot, Megan was immediately surrounded by a crowd of admiring boys, flocking to see her new toy. I left Megan to her court and walked toward the front steps, scanning the crowd for one face.

"Kit!"

He waved, and I walked faster. He'd added a layer of tan during his week on the Mississippi Gulf, and his nose was peeling. His blond hair showed the familiar cowlick at the crown, and his sweatshirt was faded. I felt a familiar rush of joy.

I wished I had the nerve to throw my arms around him, despite the people around us. Megan would have done it. I stopped on the bottom step and grinned up at him.

"It's been a long week," I told him.

Kit grinned. "Still my girl?"

"Bet on it." I stared up at him, trying to memorize the angles of his face.

Megan caught up with me and said, "Hi, Kit."

"Hello, Megan. Have a good Christmas?"

"Are you kidding? Wait till you see my new car."

"That's great, Megan," Kit said. To my relief, he was looking at me again. Kit was the only boyfriend I'd ever had who could turn back to me after seeing Megan. The old doubts died hard.

Having lost his attention, Megan's interest quickly faded. "See you later." She disappeared inside the double doors.

Kit and I lingered on the steps until the sharp clanging of the bell made me jump. "We'd better get to class," he said.

I followed him toward the door. Engulfed in the line of slow-moving students, I murmured, "You're the only boy in school who doesn't melt when Megan looks your way. How come?"

Kit grinned. "My natural good sense."

"No," I insisted. "Why?"

He leaned against a locker, waiting for the crowd in the hall to clear. "Megan reminds me of a dog we once had."

"A dog?"

"Gorgeous thing, but she'd been mistreated as a puppy. When you tried to pet her, you never knew if she would lick your hand or bite it off."

Kit's family had moved back to Rockford after his father's death. He might not know the details of the Willowby scandal, but he had sensed the truth. Some day I would tell him about Megan's mother, who had left her baby daughter to run off with another man, but not now.

"Got to run," Kit said. "See you at lunch."

"Right." I felt the familiar happiness at the thought of Kit waiting for me, then hurried down the hall.

Megan drove me home after school. When I let myself into the house, I could smell the rich aroma of beef stew. I found Mother upstairs in front of her bedroom mirror, holding up a blue dress and frowning.

"New dress?"

"No," she shook her head. "An old one. I'm trying to decide if it has any more mileage left."

"Something special coming up?"

"Maybe." She hung the dress back in the closet. "How was school?"

"Okay." I considered telling Mother about the apprehension I felt about Megan, but decided not to.

She headed for the stairs. "I have a pie in the oven."

"What are we celebrating?"

She laughed and didn't answer. I went back to my room and opened my trig book.

For dinner, not only did we have savory beef stew and corn-bread sticks, but fried okra and black-eyed peas as well, all Dad's favorites. After the plates were cleared, Mother brought out the pie.

"Pecan," Dad noted in approval. "Any more milk, hon?"

Mother stood up and went to the refrigerator. After she'd refilled his glass, she said, "Marge is going to take that real-estate course at the business school in

Thanville. It's two nights a week, seven till ten. I told her I'd go with her."

Dad put down his fork; agitation made his southern drawl more pronounced than usual. "Good *lawd*, Sue. You know I don't like you driving after dark."

Mother sounded calm. "There'll be two of us, Adam. And the highway's not exactly a back road."

"And in the winter, too." Dad didn't seem to hear. "You remember that ice storm we had last year?"

"This winter's been quite mild," Mother pointed out. "And if the weather turns bad, we could always miss a class or two. The course lasts three months."

"Three months!" Dad's jaw settled into his bulldog stance.

I put down my fork, alarmed over the brewing conflict.

"I'd like to get my real-estate license, Adam," Mother told him. "John Carris said he'll have an opening in his agency next year. When Lacey goes away to college, the house will be pretty empty. I'd like to try something new."

"What about your Sunday-school work?" Dad demanded. "And the March of

29

Dimes? You always head the annual drive. What will they think if you just drop everything?"

"I think I can manage, Adam. Besides, I thought some extra money might come in handy, with college fees and all."

I felt a stab of guilt, and Dad's face turned red. "Shoot! I guess I can afford to send my daughter to college." His voice rose. "It's not like I've got half a dozen."

The silence at the table was absolute. Mother had gone as white as Dad was red, and I stared at them both in horror, afraid to say a word. Mother pushed her chair back from the table and, without a sound, ran out of the room.

I threw Dad a reproachful glance, but he had already hurried after her. "Sue, honey, I didn't mean—that didn't come out the way I—Sue!"

Left alone, I sighed and began to clear away the dishes. Upstairs a door slammed, and I wondered if Dad was inside or outside the bedroom.

Carrying the dishes to the sink, I thought about the graveyard just outside of town, and the three small graves that marked Mother's attempts to have the big, happy family she always dreamed of. She had wanted each baby badly, and none had lived more than a few hours. Except me. That gave me a funny feeling, sometimes.

I finished the dishes and left them to drain, wiped the table and swept the floor. The house was very quiet; whatever conversation went on upstairs was inaudible. My homework was done, so I wandered into the living room and flipped on the TV. Nothing interesting. Going to the phone, I dialed Kit's number, but his little sister answered.

"Kit's at work."

I thanked her and hung up, wishing he were here to put his arms around me.

The phone rang almost as soon as I replaced the receiver. I picked it up eagerly. It was Megan.

"Want to go to the ball game tonight? We might win one for a change."

"Sure." Anything to get out of this silent house. "Be right there."

I took my jacket from the hook by the back door and ran out into the cool darkness.

When I crossed the road, Megan was

already sitting in her scarlet convertible, the radio turned up loud. "Let's go."

The wind was cold against my face, but Megan didn't seem to mind. "Heard from your dad?" I ventured.

She shook her head. "Every night I tell myself, 'This time he'll call.' But he never does. It makes me want to scream."

"I know the feeling."

"What have *you* got to be blue about?" Megan glanced at me in apparently genuine surprise. "You're the girl who has it all."

"Very funny," I said. "My parents had a big fight. Mother wants to take a class to get her real-estate license, and Dad doesn't like it."

"Talk about stupid. Doesn't he know how many women have careers today, married or not?" Megan's tone was derisive.

"Dad's old-fashioned."

"Like the rest of this jerkwater town," Megan scoffed. "Always about twenty years behind the rest of the world. We ought to get out of this place, you and me."

I thought about Kit and didn't answer.

When we reached the high school, the

gym seemed ready to overflow with spectators. We stood in line to buy our tickets. The game had already started. From the outer door, I could hear the solid thud of the ball hitting the hardwood floor, the rapid shuffle of rubber soles against wood. Cheers rang out once, then loud groans, and the shrill note of the ref's whistle.

"Hurry up," I told Megan, who had lingered to flirt with the ticket seller.

We squeezed onto the end of one of the bleachers. Our side of the gym was packed, and Red Plains High, tonight's opponent, had a good crowd also. I strained to read the scoreboard past Megan's shoulder.

Bad news. Halfway through the first quarter, Rockford trailed, sixteen to ten.

"Where's John Paul?" I heard Megan ask. "I thought he would play tonight."

"Unless his knee is still bothering him," I suggested, scanning the players' bench. John Paul sat on the end, deep in discussion with the coach.

The Rockford fans, their frustration apparent, shouted occasional encouragement from the crowded sidelines. By the end of the first quarter, we had fallen even further behind, and I wasn't the only person who watched John Paul, waiting.

Finally the coach waved to the ref and motioned a man off the court. Everyone strained to see who was being sent in. A general roar shook the bleachers when John Paul unfolded his lanky, elegant frame and walked out onto the floor.

"Now we'll show them!" Megan exulted.

I gripped both hands together. "Red Plains hasn't beaten us in ten years. We'll never hear the end of it if they win tonight."

Now it was a different game.

John Paul slipped past the other players as if they were glued to the floor. He was a dark, fluid shadow, never still, never awkward. He moved with grace and ease, and his wide hands held the ball as if it belonged only to him. With each shot the ball flew into the basket like a bird returning to its nest. On his third goal, the crowd began to chant, "Go, John Paul, go!"

Megan and I yelled, too. "Go, John Paul!" Megan jumped up and down, while I stamped my feet until we were both out of breath. It was a wonderful game.

Once, when the team paused to hear a referee explain a foul, John Paul stood briefly right in front of us. Sweat burnished his dark skin, and he breathed quickly, though his expression remained serene.

Megan stared at him as if hypnotized. I felt a stirring of unease.

Then someone touched my shoulder. I turned to see Kit grinning at me.

"Did you have to work late?"

Kit nodded. "With all the flu going around, Mr. Patton had a lot of prescriptions for me to deliver. How's the game?"

"Take a look." I nodded toward the scoreboard. "The crowd's going crazy. John Paul's going to be a big hero again."

"He should be," Kit agreed. "The college scouts are taking note of him. If he doesn't get hurt again, he'll probably be offered a scholarship. If we win the district title, he can take his pick of offers. That basketball's going to be his ticket out of Rockford."

"He needs it," I said. I thought about John Paul's family. His dad had been killed in a mill accident years ago; his mother cleaned houses and tried her best to keep her family going. A basketball scholarship was probably John Paul's only chance for college.

"Man, is he good," Kit breathed, watching the rapid play on the floor. "Look at that shot." The bleachers shook with cheers, and we shouted with the rest.

When the final buzzer sounded, the home crowd went wild, rushing onto the court. Excited fans surrounded John Paul, shaking his hand and clapping his back. John Paul smiled politely, but with restraint, not completely letting go—as if he didn't entirely trust the eager crowd of mostly white faces that milled around him.

"Can I drive you home?" Kit asked from beside me.

"I wish. I promised Megan we'd go to the Burger Pit. Can you come?"

Kit shook his head. "I've got stacks of homework."

"Sure?"

He looked torn. "Maybe for a few minutes."

I gave him a quick hug. "No, you've got a scholarship to win, too. Better go home and study."

Kit grinned, his gray-blue eyes crinkling

around the edges. "Guess I understand how John Paul feels."

He leaned forward and touched his lips to mine, then drew back and squeezed my hand. "See you tomorrow."

When I turned back to Megan, she stood at the edge of the court, watching John Paul.

"Great game, wasn't it?" I said. "We'll be back in the competition again if John Paul goes on playing."

"Yeah, sure," Megan said. "Come on, let's get something to eat. I'm starved."

I followed her through the milling crowd. "Didn't you have dinner?"

"Mrs. Frog made her tuna casserole; you've got to be desperate to eat that junk."

Once in the car, Megan started the engine with a roar, and we headed toward Rockford High's usual hangout.

Most of the tables at the Burger Pit had already filled. We stood in line to buy sodas and a burger for Megan, then found two empty chairs at the end of a table. Not deigning to talk to the freshman sitting beside her, Megan turned her chair around and looked over the small restaurant.

Jenny, one of our cheerleaders, came in the door. Catching her eye as she went by, I waved; she smiled in answer but continued past us to a table crowded with black students.

Like oil and water, I thought. You could mix the two groups together in class, but given a moment to settle, each tended to pull apart. That's the way it was in Rockford.

Megan seemed to be watching for someone. She had finished her cheeseburger and gnawed on her straw absently while she kept an eye on the door.

"The team has to shower and change," I reminded her, guessing the focus of her thoughts. "That's why they're late."

Megan just grinned. "Mind reader. Go polish your crystal ball. Look, here they come."

As the door banged open, the team walked inside as one group and headed for the largest table, empty except for a couple of underclassmen who vacated it hurriedly.

"Good game!" Megan called, and I joined in the general cheer from the rest of the room.

The ball players seated themselves around the table. John Paul and three other black guys, Tim and C.D. and the white kids, all settled on rickety chairs. The team had its own loyalties, and for the beginning of the evening, at least, would stay together.

Megan stood up.

"Going somewhere?" I asked, grinning.

Not bothering to answer, she wandered over to the next table and spoke briefly to one of the boys, who almost dropped his burger in his eagerness to reply. The girl beside him threw Megan a dirty look that Megan, true to form, ignored. She laughed at the boy's comment, then moved on to the next table.

In a seemingly casual but perfectly deliberate pattern, exchanging a few words here and there, Megan made her way across the restaurant to the table where the basketball team had settled.

I watched her, grateful that Buddy wasn't around. He might not yet be aware that Megan changed her boyfriends to coincide with the sports calendar. I thought of a phrase we had discussed in history class: The king is dead; long live the king.

Megan perched on the end of the table, curving her jean-clad body to show off her trim figure, and seemed to focus her attention on Tim Rush.

At least he wasn't going steady, and he was probably big enough to stand up to Buddy. I finished my milk shake, keeping an eye on Megan so that she didn't go off and leave me.

With nothing else to do, I watched the boys at the table as Megan laughed and talked. In a few minutes she moved to a chair, pulling it between Tim and John Paul, brushing John Paul's arm as she seated herself in the cramped quarters. John Paul drew back to give her room, and something in Megan's expression made me pause.

I almost had a glimpse of an idea, then, but it hung on the edge of my thoughts only an instant till I shook it away. I glanced at my watch, knowing I should leave, remembering the trouble at home.

Fortunately the group began to break up; several of the players had already moved to other tables or left for home. I saw John Paul and another black player head for the parking lot. Megan was still talking to

Tim, but when I started toward her, she stood up at once.

"Got to go," she told Tim. "Lacey will turn into a pumpkin at midnight."

Tim laughed, while I made a face at Megan. She followed me outside and started the car without complaint.

"What are you up to?" I demanded.

"Me?" Her gaze was innocence itself. It might have worked on the boys, but I knew her too well. "Whatever do you mean?" She drawled her words like a southern belle in a TV commercial. I gritted my teeth.

I sat in dignified silence until we pulled up in front of my house, then said, "Next time, smarty, you can go to the game by yourself."

"Oh, come on, Lacey," Megan said. "Don't be mad. I got you home on time."

"For once."

"See you tomorrow?" Her tone sounded conciliatory. "Okay?"

"I guess so," I said. "Night."

I slipped my key into the lock and stepped inside, flipping off the porch light. Then I stood for a moment in the darkness, waiting.

Sure enough, instead of pulling into her driveway, Megan turned her small car back toward town and roared zipping away into the night.

CHAPTER

FOUR

When I went down to breakfast Friday morning, Dad had already left for the office. Mother drank a cup of coffee while I ate, but she seemed lost in thought. I wondered if they had made up yet.

At school Mrs. Williams was ill, so instead of English we had an extra study hall and didn't get to begin work on the Shakespeare project she had assigned our class. At lunchtime I caught a glimpse of Megan at the table where all the athletes congregated, but I ignored her and ate lunch with

Kit. We held hands under the table while he fed me one of his french fries.

"Do you have to work tonight?" I asked.

" 'Fraid so. But Saturday I'm off at three. Want to go to a movie?"

"Can you afford it?"

"Sure."

"Why don't you come over and watch TV, and I'll make us some popcorn? Susan told me in government that the new film isn't very good anyhow."

"If that's what you want," Kit agreed. "But only if I get to kiss you at least twice during the commercials."

"Who's arguing?"

When I walked to the parking lot after school, I saw Buddy towering over the red convertible, with Megan already seated behind the wheel. Buddy leaned over her, his face dark with anger, and pointed his finger accusingly. Megan looked unimpressed. As I approached, he stalked away. I opened the car door and got in.

"What's the matter with Buddy? Did he hear about you flirting with the whole ball team Thursday night?"

"Who cares? No, he asked me out to-night. I turned him down."

"You have a date with someone else?"

To my surprise, she shook her head.

"You don't mean someone turned *you* down? History in the making?"

She flushed a little at the sarcasm in my voice. "Lay off, Lacey."

"You mean it? You've got your eye on someone who's not a pushover for you?"

"I'm not saying." Megan looked almost guilty. "You'll just give me a lecture."

"On what? Come on, spill it," I demanded.

She just shook her head.

Megan usually wasn't coy about her designs. In fact, she often boasted about her next victim. What was she up to now? And then I remembered how she had stared at John Paul the other night in the gym, and then how she had sat right next to him at the Burger Pit, and an unspoken fear stirred inside me. I tried to push it away, afraid to look it in the face.

I stared at Megan as she turned the car into the highway. "Who is it, Megan?"

She drove in silence for a long time, then

muttered. "Not yet. I'm not sure if he . . ."

I didn't have the nerve to ask again. When Megan let me out at my driveway, she said, "See you later."

I nodded and watched her turn into her own driveway. Then I walked into the house, thinking at first that no one was home. I finally located Mother in the attic, stirring up clouds of dust as she swept rigorously around stacks of old boxes.

I backed away down the narrow stairs without speaking. When Mother starts heavy cleaning, she's really upset. That fight last night must have been a dilly.

Maybe Dad would decide to make up tonight. I wondered what he would bring her. When they quarreled, he always came home with something—a box of candy, flowers. Just like in an old episode of *I Love Lucy*.

When Mother reappeared, covered in dust, I was doing trig problems at the kitchen table.

"Have a good day?" She wiped a streak of dirt off her nose.

I nodded. "Okay if Kit comes over tomorrow night to watch TV?"

"Certainly." Mother took out some potatoes and began to peel them.

"Need any help?"

She shook her head.

By the time Dad came home, savory
odors filled the kitchen, and I had set the
table. He put his coat and briefcase in the
front closet and then came into the
kitchen. He carried a small white box and
looked a bit sheepish.

Boy, I thought, *must have been a good
fight*.

He gave Mother a quick peck on the
cheek and held out his present, like a little
boy not sure if his peace offering will be
spurned.

Mother accepted the box, but her smile
seemed strained. While she opened it, I
came and peeked over her shoulder.

It was a pin, in the shape of a leaf. Quite
pretty, I thought.

"Thank you, Adam." Mother sounded
subdued.

But Dad cheered up visibly. "I made a
big insurance sale to a farmer in the next
county," he told us. "Shoot, the commis-
sion from this policy alone will put me
over the top for the month."

"That's nice," Mother said, her voice quiet.

After dinner Dad went into the den to watch TV, and I helped Mother clear the table.

"Are you still angry?" I asked her.

"Angry isn't the right word, Lacey." She slipped dishes into the soapy water. "I just wish he could understand why I want to do this." She stared out through the small window as if seeing past the barren winter garden. "When we were first married, the local high school offered adult classes at night. They had a beginner's course in auto mechanics, and I wanted to sign up."

"That doesn't surprise me," I said as I reached for another dish to wipe dry. If anything broke at our house, it was Mother who did the fixing. "You've got a real knack with a screwdriver. Give Dad a hammer and he ends up with a swollen thumb and an increased vocabulary."

Mother smiled briefly. "Your father had a fit," she went on. " 'My wife out at night with all those men,' he said. 'What does a woman need to know about car engines!' He made such a fuss that I didn't go. I've always regretted that."

48

"That's sad," I said.

She rinsed out the sink while I wiped off the counter, trying to imagine my mother and father not much older than me. When I turned to leave, Mother said, "The realtor's class starts Tuesday night, Lacey. I'll put something in the oven for dinner. You can take it out after school and clean up afterwards."

"You're still going to go?" I couldn't hide my surprise.

"Yes. This time I'm going through with it."

I thought about Dad at dinner, relaxed and making jokes, obviously thinking that she had dropped the idea. Oh, boy.

"Go for it," I said.

Saturday I slept late and spent the afternoon doing laundry. I gave myself a facial and tried my hair in a different style, determined to be extra pretty for Kit.

I expected him by six-thirty, but it was past seven when he knocked on our door.

I ran to let him in. Kit stood up straight in the doorway this time. He looked tired; even his smile seemed to take great effort.

"Sorry I'm late."

"That's okay." I stepped aside, expecting a quick kiss, but he walked on toward the den. What was wrong?

We went into the den together, and Kit said hello to my parents. Dad was absorbed in his favorite detective show.

"Like some popcorn?" I asked.

"Sure."

Kit followed me into the kitchen. While I poured oil into a heavy kettle and added a handful of corn, he leaned on the edge of the counter.

"Something wrong at work?"

He shook his head. "A lot of deliveries today."

"Mr. Patton in a bad mood?"

"He's okay."

Something wasn't okay. "Did your little sister get over her sore throat?" Kit felt responsible toward his family; he'd grown up in a hurry when his dad died.

"She's better."

I reached for a plastic bowl, then, as the first kernel exploded inside the kettle, turned back to shake the pan.

The corn rattled the lid of the kettle in a crescendo of staccato pops. Kit didn't speak until I moved the kettle off the heat and began to pour the popped corn into the bowls.

"Carla called," he told me.

"Your sister?"

He nodded. "The baby has the croup, and Sam's on night shift. She didn't know what to do."

"I guess your mother's advice helped."

Kit reached for the salt shaker, and I took some soft drinks out of the refrigerator. Hands full, we headed back for the den.

My parents ate some popcorn, then Mother went upstairs, and in a few minutes Dad followed. Now that we were alone in the den, I shifted closer to Kit on the couch and hoped that he would put his arm around my shoulders.

He didn't move.

"What's with you?" I blurted. "Somebody build a wall between us?"

"Huh?" Kit frowned at me. "I didn't do anything."

"I noticed." I couldn't keep the irritation out of my voice. "If you're angry at me, just say so."

"I'm not mad. Don't get all upset over nothing."

"This isn't nothing!" My voice had risen. "You've ignored me all night."

"I wasn't ignoring you; I've just got some things on my mind, that's all." He wouldn't meet my eyes—Kit, who was always so open and honest. I could feel tension building inside me; the muscles in my neck felt taut and hard. Something was wrong, and he didn't want to tell me.

"What things?" I demanded.

"Have you sent off your college applications yet?"

"Sure," I told him, "the same time you did, don't you remember?"

"You still plan on being a pediatrician?"

I stared at him, bewildered by the change in topic. "I've always wanted to be a pediatrician, Kit. Why should I change my mind?"

He shrugged. "No reason. But I'm glad."

"Why?" He was making no sense at all.

"I think you'll make a good one." At last he moved his arm to circle my shoulders and pulled me closer. He kissed me once lightly, and I laid my head against his shoulder. We watched the flickering screen together, but I could feel his distraction.

At eleven Kit stood up. "I'd better be going."

"Kit," I began, my mouth almost too dry to speak, then lost my nerve. I wanted to ask, "Don't you care for me anymore?" but I was afraid to hear his answer.

He put his arms around me. I leaned against his chest, trying to find the old contentment, hoping that my fears would vanish like murky visions from a fading dream. But the lines of worry still creased his forehead.

"I only want what's best for you," he murmured into my hair.

"You're the best for me," I whispered.

But he released me too soon, and I saw him frown.

At the door he gave me a quick kiss, then walked rapidly toward his car.

What had happened to Kit, to Kit and me?

I turned out the lights and locked the door, then slowly climbed the stairs. In my room I stared into the mirror for a long time. No matter how long I stared, I couldn't take my round face and make it slim and soulful; my brown hair was still ordinary, not blond and long and graceful.

My eyes would always be brown, not a clear blue.

I thought I'd outgrown those feelings. I hadn't.

CHAPTER

FIVE

Megan picked me up as usual Monday morning, but neither of us seemed eager to talk. She drove more slowly than normal, her eyes on the road. I stared at my books, once sneaking a quick glance at Megan. What would it be like to attract boys without even trying? To have them lining up eagerly, overcome by your Siren's charms? I'd never know. And the Siren herself seemed hardly ecstatic.

Just once, couldn't we switch places? I thought. *Why was Megan born to be beautiful, and why do I have to feel sec-ond best?* I could feel bitterness heavy inside me.

I hadn't been able to talk to Kit on Sunday; he'd spent the whole day helping Mr. Patton take inventory. Kit usually waited for me at the front of the school, but today he wasn't there. I went off to class feeling about as desirable as a gorilla.

I didn't see Megan again until English class. Mrs. Williams was back, coughing and hacking. The first thing she did was split the class into small groups and instruct us to choose a scene from one of Shakespeare's plays to perform. Megan was assigned to my group, as was Sue Ann, David, Ron—and John Paul.

Megan seemed unusually absorbed in our little project. She argued with Sue Ann about whether to choose a comedy or a tragedy, while the boys discussed our team's chances of making district finals.

I just sat lost in my own black cloud.

When the lunch bell rang, I picked up my books and headed for my locker, not waiting for Megan. She caught up with me at the head of the stairs.

"Some friend you are," she huffed, out of

breath from running. "You're the straight-A kid. You could have helped me out a little."

I didn't answer.

"Hey, are you mad at me, Lacey?"

"Why should I be mad?" I could hardly explain the irrational resentment that burned inside me, just because Megan was Megan, and I was still plain old Lacey.

I saw Kit waiting at the cafeteria door.

"Long time no see," he said.

I searched for guilt in his smile, for evidence of boredom politely veiled. But he looked like the same adorable Kit.

"Coming to eat with us, Megan?" Kit asked as I tried to read his face.

"No, thanks." Megan headed toward the front of the long room where the athletes sat.

"Say hi to Tim," I told her.

"What? Oh, yeah."

I gave Kit a searching look. "I didn't see you this morning."

"Ellen had to take her science project to school, so I drove her over; she didn't think all the tubes and jars would fit on the bus."

As simple as that; his little sister in need of a ride. Maybe I had worried for nothing.

But what about his strange mood Saturday night? I tried to push my troubling doubts away.

"Are you hungry?"

"Starved."

"Better head for the cheeseburgers," Kit suggested. "They're probably cold already."

We both grinned, trying to ease the stiffness between us. But he didn't take my hand, and I knew that the wall was still there.

Tuesday I got to English class early, resigned to an hour of listening to our group butcher Shakespeare's immortal lines. Megan was already there. She had cornered John Paul outside the classroom and was talking earnestly to him. Finally he nodded, and Megan beamed. What was going on?

I found out soon enough. The rest of the class moved into the groups, and Megan slipped inside the door just as the bell rang.

"Where's John Paul?" David asked.

"Went to the library to get a book." Megan wore an air of suppressed triumph.

I stared at her suspiciously.

"I told Mrs. Williams that we're going to do *Othello*."

"What?" I said. "I thought you were talking about one of the comedies."

"But Megan," Sue Ann wailed. "I don't have Cliffs Notes for *Othello*!"

"Don't worry." Megan's tone was breezy. "We'll find you one. John Paul said he would take the lead."

"He did?" I asked in surprise. John Paul was very shy off the basketball court.

Megan nodded. "I told him we really needed him; none of the other boys can read their way out of a paper bag."

"Thanks a lot," Ron muttered.

"And I need a good grade on this in the worst way," Megan added virtuously.

"Since when have you started worrying about grades?" I demanded.

"What are you complaining about? You're the one who always gives me lectures—'Get with it, Megan, or you'll never graduate with the rest of us.' Remember?"

"And you're actually listening?"

John Paul returned, and we settled down to attack the play. Megan gave us a quick summary of the plot; she had actually read the whole play Monday night. That

surprised me so much that again I wondered what was going on.

"It's this Moor, you see, who marries
Desdemona. But this guy Iago doesn't like
her. He plants a handkerchief in the lieutenant's room, and Othello thinks Desdemona's fooling around with the other guy,
and he kills her."

"Over a *handkerchief*!" Sue Ann's eyes
widened.

Ron and David began to argue over who
should play Iago. Nobody had any doubts
as to who Desdemona would be.

"Sue Ann, you can be the serving
woman. Lacey doesn't want to act; she'll
introduce the skit and give a plot summary."

Megan moved her chair next to John
Paul's and began to discuss how to con-
dense a short scene for the class presenta-
tion.

"I'm going to the library to look for a
copy of *Othello*," I said. Sue Ann decided
to come with me. The other two boys had
forgotten the play entirely and were dis-
cussing when duck season would open.
Too bad. This time I would let Megan do
the worrying.

* * *

When I got home Tuesday, I found a note from Mother in the kitchen. "Put casserole in at 5:00; cook at 350 degrees for one hour."

Great. I had forgotten about Mother's evening class. Dad would be in a foul mood.

Sure enough, he came in about ten past six, looked at the table set only for two, and demanded, "Where's your mother?"

"Her class, remember?"

His expression darkened.

We ate in silence, and I was glad when I could clear the table.

On impulse I went to the phone and dialed Kit's number. When I heard his voice, relief flooded through me. "Kit?"

"Something wrong?"

"Yes and no. Think we could take a drive or something?"

"I'm really snowed under with homework, Lacey."

"That's okay," I lied. But the weight of my anger and frustration seemed too heavy to bear alone. Everything was a mess. "No, it's not," I said. "I need to get out of the house, and I need to talk to you."

For a moment I didn't think he would answer. "Okay, but I can't stay out very long," he said finally. "I'll be there in ten minutes."

"Great."

I finished the dishes in record time, then took my jacket off its peg by the back door. I found Dad sitting in the den in front of the TV.

"I'm going out for a little while."

His expression didn't change; I'm not even sure he heard me.

Shaking my head, I went to the front door to watch for Kit. When he drove up, I ran outside and slipped into the car. "Hi."

He nodded as he backed the car out of the drive. "Where do you want to go?"

"I don't care; I just want to get away from this house."

He hesitated a moment, then turned the little car toward Main Street.

I tried to bury a flicker of irrational disappointment. There was an almost deserted street on the opposite side of town where the high-school kids went to park. Kit and I had had some sessions there, but we'd agreed to avoid it in the future. Not that we didn't enjoy making out, but after awhile it had gotten too difficult to stop.

I knew avoiding Lovers' Lane was the right thing to do—the smart thing to do—but still, I missed those long kisses, the feeling of being almost one. That was what marriage would be like, I guessed, when nobody would have to pull away. Did Kit ever wonder about what we were missing?

At the Dairy Stop, he pulled into the parking lot. "Want a Coke?"

I nodded.

He slid out behind the wheel and walked up to the window. In a moment he came back with two paper cups filled with cola.

I took a sip. The soft drink stung my tongue slightly, but the cold liquid felt good against the back of my throat.

"So, what's up?"

I poked my straw around in the soda. "My dad's being a real pain. Mother went to her first realtor's class tonight, and he's so mad he won't even talk to *me*."

Kit shrugged. "He'll get over it. Don't worry so much."

"Easy for you to say," I fumed. "Men are such hard heads! Always wanting their way. And not even being honest about it!"

"Hey, you don't have to take it out on me." Kit looked up from his Coke, frowning.

"Why not?" It felt so good to finally put my anger into words that I didn't want to stop. "Aren't you the same way?"

"About what?" Kit looked genuinely confused.

"You've had something on your mind all week, and you won't tell me what's wrong."

His puzzled expression faded, and he looked away from me. "Nothing's wrong."

"See?" I pulled so hard on my straw that the ice rattled against the almost-empty cup. "Something *is* wrong, but you don't want to talk about it!"

"Lacey, I don't have anything to say. I've just got a lot on my mind, that's all."

"But there is something."

Kit's lips folded into a hard line. "It's nothing to do with you."

"Anything that bothers you affects me, because I care about you," I told him. "Don't you understand that?"

He shifted in his seat. "Lacey—"

"What?"

"You know all those plans we made?"

"What plans?" I knew that I sounded bitter.

Kit stared at me as if I'd lost all my wits. "You know, college."

"Oh, that." We'd spent hours poring over college catalogs, everything from Jackson State to Ol' Miss, which Kit called the "impossible dream" because of its high fees. "Sure."

We'd surveyed every college that had a premed degree for me and a pharmacy program for Kit. Pharmacy had always interested him, and Mr. Patton had promised him a job after he graduated. I suspected the drugstore owner, with no children of his own, would be happy to make Kit a partner eventually.

A new thought struck me, and I turned to Kit, feeling suddenly anxious. "Kit! You didn't hear about your scholarship?"

If he'd lost the scholarship, there'd be plenty of reason for his being distracted.

Kit shook his head. "No, I haven't heard anything yet."

"You'll get it," I assured him. "I know you will. We're going to make it, and we'll do it together."

Kit grinned, but his smile looked

unconvincing. "I guess. If your dad doesn't insist on you going to Columbus so you can be cloistered."

"The Mississippi University for Women? Fat chance!" I told him. "That was Dad's idea of a joke. I'm going where you go. We applied to the same colleges, didn't we?"

He nodded, but he looked morose again. "At least you've got your family to help you. I've got to make my way by myself. Even if I get the scholarship, it won't pay for everything. Working part-time and keeping my grades up, I won't have time for much else."

"So?" I glared at him, feeling unfairly accused. "I understand that. I don't expect the moon."

Yet that wasn't quite true. I *did* want something more. I wanted him to put into words what he felt about me. I wanted to know if he still saw us together beyond high school, even beyond college.

I remembered Christmas Eve, when he gave me the locket. For one moment I thought the small jeweler's box might contain a ring, and my heart had soared. Of course I knew it was too soon to make those kinds of plans. My mind knew that, but another part of me still hungered for a more definite commitment and thoughts about wedding dresses and small apartments and even cribs someday.

"I just don't need any more pressure on me, that's all," Kit muttered, breaking into my thoughts.

I felt my cheeks flame. "Pardon me for living," I snapped. "Look, I don't want to interfere with your studying. We'd better go."

I wanted him to disagree.

Instead he nodded, glancing at his watch. "I've got a report to finish and a big chem test tomorrow."

"As long as we know what's important," I said, as he put the car into gear.

"Now, look, I just said—"

"Oh, please," I told him. "Take me home."

We drove home in silence. I got out of the car quickly, without kissing him goodbye, and ran up to the porch. But I stopped there, leaning against the post as the little VW pulled away. I watched it disappear down the lane before I walked into the house.

* * *

For the rest of the week, the atmosphere at home continued to be tense. My parents didn't argue, and sometimes I thought that a loud quarrel might be a relief. They were so formal and polite to each other that it set my nerves on edge. The laughter had gone from our house, and with it the easy warmth full of love and understanding. It made me think uneasily of all the kids I knew whose parents were divorced. Sometimes I couldn't sleep at night, worrying. Suddenly nothing seemed stable or sure, not my parents, not my relationship with Kit, not Megan. . . .

I would have liked to talk to Mother, but the right moment never came. She worked extra hard around the house, and our dinners would have won prizes at the county fair. But I had little appetite.

Friday morning when Megan came to pick me up, her eyes were shining.

"Tim called me last night!"

"And?"

"The basketball team is having a party after the game tonight at Mitch Swanson's house. By invitation only."

I glanced at the smile she was trying to

swallow. "And you were honored with an invitation."

"Right." She took the turn into the highway with a spurt of speed that made me catch my breath.

"If you don't slow down, you won't live until tonight," I grumbled. Megan, in unusually high spirits, ignored me.

Her happiness was short-lived. After first period I was on my way to chemistry class when I saw a crowd by the side door. When the mass of students parted for an instant, I recognized Buddy's broad back. He had someone pinned against the wall. I pushed through to get a closer look.

It was Buddy, all right. Even from the side I could see the anger that turned his thick neck red and tightened his small mouth. Tim, his face pale as he tried to conceal his fear, struggled in Buddy's grip.

"Remember what I told you, you skinny wimp." Buddy lifted the lighter boy and thrust him back against the concrete block wall.

We all heard the crack as Tim's head hit the wall. His eyes rolled in his head as if he were about to pass out. But when Buddy released him, Tim sagged but didn't fall.

The crowd of students shifted as Buddy stalked past. No one had the nerve to protest, but some looked upset.

"Tim!" I said. "Are you okay?"

His face was still pale, but now another emotion — humiliation, probably — overcame his fear. He tried to smile. "Sure," he muttered. "That clown doesn't scare me."

Tim disappeared into the boys' rest room, and I hurried on to class. Later in the morning, I found Megan waiting for me by the English classroom.

"Is it true?" She grabbed my arm, almost knocking my books out of my hand. "About Buddy and Tim?"

"You should have seen it," I told her. "What's with Buddy, anyhow? He think he's the KKK or something?"

Megan's face contorted with anger. "If he thinks he's going to get me back by pushing my friends around, he's dumber than I thought."

"Have you talked to Buddy? Told him it's over between you two?"

"I told him I didn't want to go out anymore. What do I have to do—take out an ad? He doesn't own me!"

I shook my head.

"Well?" Megan demanded.

"I was just wondering who you'll have left to go out with," I said. "I wouldn't count on Tim, not after this morning. The other boys may have second thoughts, too. Buddy's not the kind of guy anyone wants for an enemy."

"I wish Buddy would sink into the Delta and rot!" Megan added a few more blunt words that made me glance uneasily toward the door.

"The teacher'll hear you," I warned. "Come on, class is starting."

After another hour rehearsing our skit, we headed for the lunchroom. "Are you eating lunch with Tim?"

"Of course." Megan tossed her blond hair defiantly.

Megan ate at the athletes' table, but Tim didn't show up for lunch at all, and the other boys didn't rush around her as usual. Buddy watched her with possessive eyes. Megan ignored him as thoroughly as a hound who refuses to scratch a persistent flea.

At our table Kit seemed distracted. I chewed on a cold grilled-cheese sandwich and said, "I wonder if Megan's finally met someone as stubborn as she is."

Kit shrugged. "Buddy's a sorehead, but he'll cool off sooner or later."

I shook my head. "I don't know; I think there's going to be trouble."

CHAPTER

SIX

Friday afternoon Megan didn't mention the basketball party, and I hoped that she had dropped the idea. If she gave Buddy a chance to cool off, maybe he would stop acting like such an ape.

I was in my room dressing when the phone rang.

"Lacey," Kit's familiar voice said. "Mr. Patton wants me to work a few more hours. Do you mind?"

"No," I said slowly. "That's okay."

"Go ahead to the game, if you like. I'll come by your house later."

"Sure." I hung up the receiver reluctantly. In less than a minute it rang again.

"Lacey?" Megan said. "Are you going to the basketball game with Kit?"

"No," I told her. "He's working again. Same old story."

"Rough. Come with me, then. I'll be ready in fifteen minutes."

It was more like thirty. By the time she drove up, I knew we'd missed the beginning of the game.

"What are you all dressed up for?" I pointed to her creamy silk blouse and new jeans.

"The party, of course." She tossed her long hair; I could see that she was wearing more make-up than usual.

"You're just asking for trouble, Megan," I warned. "Give Buddy more time to get used to being dumped. He's usually the one who breaks up with his girls, you know."

"Listen." Megan backed the car out of our drive. "That jerk can't run my life."

Cars and pickup trucks crowded the school parking lot. We bought our tickets and walked into the gym. A noisy crowd packed the bleachers. Attendance had slipped during our losing streak; now it looked like old times. Rockford High was back on top, and the whole town had turned out to cheer.

Megan and I found a spot at the end of the bleachers and squeezed into the mass of spectators. I watched the boys running up and down the hardwood floor. I tried to locate Tim, but I didn't see him. Megan didn't seem perturbed by his absence.

"Look!" She grabbed my arm. "John Paul's got the ball."

He leapt upward, graceful as a ballet dancer, and the ball zipped through the air, meeting the basket cleanly. The crowd roared.

"Way to go," Megan yelled. We both clapped hard.

Tim finally came into the game in the third quarter. He seemed off his form, missed several shots at the basket, then lost a recovery. The coach called him out before the quarter was over. Did Tim have Buddy on his mind?

Big Bad Buddy. The cheerleaders had chanted it during football games. The nickname had seemed cute, then. It didn't sound so cute anymore.

As if his name had conjured up the big football player, I saw Buddy across the crowded gym, standing by one of the exits. He held a paper cup in his hand and was staring at Megan.

The expression on his face made me pause. I recognized that lonely, forlorn look. I had seen it on a lot of boys when Megan winged her casual way in and out of their lives.

So it wasn't just piqued male ego. Buddy really had it bad for Megan. For a moment I felt genuinely sorry for him.

Then another cheer erupted from the crowd. I lost sight of Buddy as he stepped back into the mass of people milling around the end of the bleachers.

"Lacey," Megan breathed beside me. "Watch the way he moves."

I thought maybe Tim had come back into the game, but when I looked toward the court, John Paul had the ball. I thought about what Kit had said, that if we won the district tournament, John Paul would be assured a scholarship. It would probably be his only chance for college, and he deserved it. I prayed that nothing—or no one —would stand in his way.

"John Paul's really cool," I said casually. And then carefully, I added, "Too bad you can't go out with him."

"Yeah," Megan whispered, still intent on the game.

We won the game by a good margin, and the crowd's cheers echoed through the gymnasium. Megan's cheeks were flushed, her eyes bright. I had never seen her so elated over a ball game before, not even when she and Buddy were going steady and Buddy had made a winning touchdown. I guessed that she was caught up in the excitement of the basketball team's improved chances. But still—

"Megan," I said, under cover of the noise around us. "I don't think you should go to that party tonight."

"What?" Megan leaned closer to hear me. The crowd still yelled and stamped their feet as the home team disappeared into the locker room.

"I said, I don't think you should go. Buddy—"

"*That* to Buddy." She made a rude gesture that I was thankful he wasn't around to see. Since he had disappeared into the crowd, I hadn't seen him again. Maybe he'd gone home.

"But—"

"Nobody tells me whom to date, Lacey." Megan sounded impatient. "Come on. I've got to wait for Tim to shower and change. He told me he'd meet me in front of the school. Come wait with me, then you can drive my car home."

"Okay," I agreed reluctantly. "Just don't say I didn't warn you."

Eventually the cars began to clear out, the bus with the rival team pulled away, and Megan drove her convertible to the front of the school to wait for Tim.

"Should be a good party," she was telling me. "Mitch has a big family room, so we can dance. Dare me to dance with every member of the team?"

"All of them?"

"Sure."

"Megan, if you don't learn to stick to one guy, you're never going to—"

"Enough already," Megan snapped. "No more lectures, please."

"Fine. Be a lamebrain."

Megan bit her lip, and some of the inner

uncertainty that pushed her on showed briefly in her expression.

When she looked like a lost little girl, I couldn't stay angry. Funny, Megan was two months older than me, but I was the one who always ended up "mothering."

Maybe she'd behave at the party. Maybe the moon would turn purple.

I wished Tim would at least hurry up; I wanted to get home to Kit. The parking lot was almost deserted. Surely Tim had had time to change by now.

But the driveway in front of the school remained empty. We stared into the darkness, each lost in her own thoughts. I thought about Megan, how stubborn she was, and about Kit, and how stubborn *he* was. And then I thought about Mother and Dad, and how each of them was being stubborn, too. And then I thought about me. . . .

A sound of footsteps made Megan turn eagerly, and I sat up straight. But it was only the two boys who acted as team managers. They headed for a blue van, and then the walkway was empty again.

I think Megan and I had the same

thought. I saw her eyes go big and her mouth tighten.

"I'm going to the gym to see what's taking him so long."

"Wait for me," I said automatically.

She jumped out of the car and slammed the door. I hurried after her; she walked swiftly, despite her high-heeled boots and tight jeans.

When we rounded the corner of the school, Megan took a deep breath. No lights showed in the rear wing of the school, and the parking lot appeared deserted. Despite the evidence, Megan hurried on toward the back door and tugged on the door handle. It didn't budge.

"Locked!" Megan's voice was hoarse with anger. "He did it on purpose—told me to wait in front so I wouldn't see him leave. That jerk—" She swore briskly. I couldn't see her face in the darkness, but the note of hysteria in her voice made me shiver.

I could think of half a dozen times when Megan had stood up whatever boy she was currently dating. But no one had ever stood up Megan.

"Come on." She turned back toward the car, her steps quick.

I ran to catch up. "Megan, you're being stupid. Let him go."

But she hardly gave me time to slide into the seat before she started the engine, pulling the small car out of the front lot with a squeal of tires.

"Have you lost your mind?" I yelled.

I thought she would drive wildly straight through the fence, but she turned the car toward the rear exit. For a moment I had a glimpse of a pickup truck in the alley behind the school. The vehicle was dark, and I couldn't see a driver.

Megan turned so sharply into the road that I thought the car would flip over. I held my breath. In our rearview mirror the dark truck suddenly came alive with light. But Megan's driving left no room for any other thought, and I straightened quickly.

"Megan, slow down!"

I was so thankful when she eased up on the gas that only then did I realize we weren't headed for home.

"Hey," I said sharply. "Where are we going?"

"To the party, where else?"

"Are you nuts?"

"Nobody gets away with walking out on me," Megan muttered. "I want to look Tim Rush in the eye and watch him squirm."

"What about the time you sneaked off to the county fair and left Bert McAvoy waiting in front of your house with two tickets to the school play?"

"That was different."

"How?"

"Five minutes, just five minutes, Lacey, *please*. Let me tell Tim what I think of him, then we'll go."

She sounded calmer, and her driving was more controlled. I had time to worry about Kit, waiting at home. But short of wrestling the steering wheel away from her, I didn't have much of a choice but to go along.

We turned into a quiet side street. Half a dozen cars were parked in front of Mitch's house. Megan, noticing Tim's little compact, made a sharp sound under her breath.

I felt embarrassed. "Megan, we can't just walk into a private party. Mitch's parents will think we're crashing."

"I was *invited*," Megan said through clenched teeth.

But when she got out of the car, she hesitated. The front door was brightly lit by the porch light. Instead of walking up the front path, Megan headed around the house. With a sinking heart, I followed.

Light flooded from inside the house through open curtains. We could see the crowd inside—basketball players and their dates. The beat of a popular song floated past the glass panes, bursts of laughter punctuating its rhythm.

Sliding glass doors opened onto the patio; Megan headed toward them. She slid open the door and walked inside without ceremony. I slipped in behind her, wishing I were invisible.

Only a couple of boys noticed Megan's arrival. The group on the other side of the room was laughing and talking. Almost all the team were there. Several black players and their girls formed a small insular group at one of the card tables. The other players were clustered around the stereo. Tim had his arm around one of the cheerleaders.

I looked around for Mitch's parents, but didn't see any adults. Megan picked up a paper cup full of fruit punch from the table, then walked deliberately across the room.

"Hello, Tim," she said.

Tim's face paled. Donna, the cheerleader, stepped out of the circle of his arm.

"We *had* a date tonight." Megan's tone was deceptively sweet. She took a sip of punch. "I'm sure you wouldn't forget something like that."

The noise in the room faded. It was easy to hear Tim's reply, though he spoke softly.

"Megan, I—" He paused to swallow hard. "I didn't want to cause you any trouble. If you and Buddy—"

"Forget Buddy," Megan interrupted. "I'm through with him."

From where I stood, I could see Megan's profile. She had her head thrown back; her long golden hair glinted under the light, and her back was straight. Did she know the picture she presented—the cream-colored blouse rising and falling over her breasts, the arrogant tilt of her hips, her long legs in their tight jeans? Some of Tim's old enthusiasm seemed to return; he grinned at her.

"Who said we were through?" The harsh voice startled the whole room. Buddy's burly figure filled the doorway.

I thought of the dark truck behind the school. Buddy must have followed us and entered unnoticed while everyone watched Megan and Tim. And he had heard everything.

The tremor in his voice seemed only partly due to anger. Underneath I could hear echoes of wounded pride, and perhaps even the remnants of real affection—slighted now, which only deepened his rage.

"Who said we were through?" he repeated.

Megan, eyes bright and cheeks flushed, stepped forward to confront him.

"I did."

"I don't have anything to say about it?" A muscle in Buddy's cheek jerked.

I looked around. Tim had slipped silently out through the hall. Smart guy.

"You don't tell me what to do!" Megan's tone was savage.

Buddy half raised his arm. Megan didn't step backwards, but her eyes narrowed.

"You think that's all that matters,

Megan? What *you* want? We're not through till *I* say so. Stay and party with your friends, but don't mark me off your list so easily. I'm not finished yet."

He reached out—whether to strike her or caress her was unclear; maybe not even Buddy knew. Finally, he shoved her, and the red punch splashed over her whole body.

Megan gasped, dropping her purse as the liquid hit her. Her comb and keys and lipstick clattered on the hardwood floor. The rest of the kids froze while Buddy walked out the same way he'd come.

Megan stood still. The red liquid dripped down her cream-colored blouse. Was she going to cry? But Megan never cried. She stood alone in the center of the floor, and no one in the crowd stepped forward to help.

I reached blindly toward the buffet table for paper napkins and missed the first movement from the only boy in the room big enough to offer Megan a simple gesture of courtesy and compassion. John Paul, his expression grave, picked up the purse and its scattered contents and handed them to

Megan without a word. The rest of the kids, faces stiff, simply watched.

Megan swayed. John Paul steadied her, and she leaned briefly against his arm.

Then I reached her, wiping uselessly at her ruined blouse with the napkins.

"Are you okay?"

"Sure." Megan's face looked pale as spun cotton, but her voice sounded hard. "Let's go."

No one spoke as we walked out into the darkness. Once beyond the betraying light, I could feel Megan begin to tremble.

"Cowards," she murmured.

When we reached the car, I said, "Do you want me to drive?"

She shook her head and slipped behind the wheel. She had stopped trembling.

"Let's go home," I urged.

To my relief, she nodded.

We rode home in silence. Kit's battered VW wasn't parked in my driveway when we got there.

I'd been sure he would wait. I forgot about Megan, slipping out of the car without a word and hurrying into the house.

Mother sat on the couch, reading her textbook.

"Did Kit come by?"

"He waited almost an hour." She didn't look up from her work. "It wasn't very considerate of you not to let him know you'd gone somewhere else, Lacey."

Great. I walked up the stairs with leaden feet, my heart even heavier. Why was *everything* going wrong?

CHAPTER

SEVEN

Saturday morning I slept late and woke feeling heavy-eyed and sluggish. Then the events of the night before came crashing back. I grabbed a robe and headed for the phone. But with my hand on the cool plastic receiver, I hesitated. I wanted to talk to Kit face-to-face.

Jumping into some clothes, I grabbed an apple as I went through the kitchen, then pulled my old ten-speed out of the garage. Maybe a ride in the cool air would clear my head.

By the time I had pedaled my way to Kit's house, my shoulders felt tense. Would he be angry about last night, thinking I had stood him up?

I walked up to the small yellow house, took a deep breath, and knocked.

To my surprise, a girl about my age opened the door.

"Carla?"

I hadn't seen Kit's sister since she had dropped out of school last year. Even so, I recognized her at once, though she had cut her hair and her eyelids were puffy and red.

"What are you—I mean, nice to see you. How's the baby?"

"Fine. Getting bigger every day." Carla sounded listless. "Looking for Kit?"

I nodded. "Is he home?"

"Just a minute." She left the door ajar and called Kit's name.

After a minute or two, Kit appeared in the doorway. He didn't motion me inside, as usual. Instead he shut the door behind him, nodding toward the wooden porch swing.

I sat down, and the rusty springs groaned.

"Kit, I'm sorry about last night." My

words tumbled out. "I didn't mean to be so late."

"That's all right." He sounded absent-minded. "I can't come study with you this afternoon, Lacey. Carla's here with the baby."

I didn't mind that he had to stay home, but I wished he sounded more regretful. "Is Carla okay?"

He nodded, without meeting my eyes. "What happened to you last night, anyhow?"

"It was Megan."

Kit grimaced. "Isn't it always? She's going to get you in real trouble someday, Lacey."

"She wouldn't do that." I tried to sound as if I believed my own words. "Tim Rush stood her up. Buddy's acting like some small-time hood, and Tim's spooked. So Megan decided to go to the basketball party anyhow, to confront Tim, and I couldn't back out, not then."

"Enjoy it?"

I made a face. "It was awful. Buddy showed up and pushed Megan around. That guy scares me, Kit."

"I wouldn't want to be in the ring with

Buddy," Kit agreed. "I think you should let Megan handle her own problems, Lacey."

"Probably. But everybody needs someone on her side," I murmured. "And Megan's so alone."

Kit put his arm around my shoulders. "That's my Lacey, bighearted as always."

His tone was hard to read; it held both tenderness and frustration. I looked up at him. Then from inside the house I heard the baby crying.

Kit stiffened. "I'd better go. I'll see you at school Monday."

"Sure." I felt somehow abandoned, though I tried to tell myself that was silly. Still, the ride home seemed very long.

I spent the rest of the day sprawled across my bed, trying to study, but more often lost in daydreams about Kit. After a silent, tasteless dinner with my folks, I finally remembered Megan. Had she recovered from last night's humiliation?

A sharp twinge of guilt assailed me; I should have called her earlier. I looked across the road at the big house behind the hedge. Had she gone out tonight? If so, with whom? I decided to walk across the road and find out.

It took only a minute to cross the street and slip around the house. The red convertible was parked behind the house, and I could see a light up in Megan's bedroom.

I considered throwing a rock at her window, just for meanness, but Megan probably wouldn't notice. I could hear strains of loud music through the thin glass.

I had to knock three times before Mrs. Frogmorton answered. The gray-haired, stocky woman stared at me, unsmiling. I couldn't remember ever seeing her smile. Stan Willowby was so desperate for housekeepers that he would take anyone who could live with Megan. Two years ago he had hired a closet alcoholic, and nobody discovered her secret till she fell asleep with a lit cigarette and almost ignited the house.

It was my dad who pulled the poor woman from the fire. Megan hadn't been home at the time.

"Is Megan here?" I asked.

The woman nodded; her glum expression a permanent fixture on the long face. "Upstairs."

I climbed the stairs slowly. No wonder Megan spent as little time as possible at home. Living with that sour-faced woman couldn't be any picnic.

I knocked at the bedroom door, but the music was too loud for her to hear. I pushed the door open and walked inside.

When Megan saw me, her expression lightened. I felt guilty again for not checking on her sooner. She sat cross-legged on the bed, her chin on her upturned palms.

"You okay?"

"Bored out of my tree," she drawled. "Can you believe—*me* sitting home on Saturday night."

I laughed. "Maybe in a few days Buddy will cool off, and you can get back to normal."

"Buddy's a pain in the—"

When I refused to blink at her string of profanities, Megan subsided. "How come you're not out with Kit?"

"Family problems."

"His or yours?"

"Both, sort of."

She crossed her arms, her expression hard to read.

"You're moving away from me, Lacey," she said abruptly. "Leaving me behind. It scares me."

"How can you say that?" I asked in genuine surprise. "You've partied with half the boys in the county, while I sat home and watched reruns. And you think *I'm* leaving *you*?"

"That stuff—it didn't mean anything," she muttered. "This is serious. You're really in love, and Kit loves you back."

"Maybe," I told her, sighing. "I hope so."

A flicker of despair crossed Megan's face. "I'd like to be in love," she whispered.

I shook my head. "Remember Jack Teller?"

"Who?"

"When we were in the ninth grade, dummy. He was a senior."

"Oh, yeah," Megan nodded. "He went off to college and never came back to Rockford. Smart guy."

"I had this terrific crush on him," I reminded her. "Couldn't think of anything else for weeks. I used to hang around his homeroom at break, just to see him walk by. One Monday he actually smiled at me. I lived on that for days."

"So?" Megan's eyes were half-shut, like a sleepy cat.

"So the next week, I managed to sit at

95

the end of his table in study hall. I'd practiced this cute little speech that would make him pay attention to me."

"Did you chicken out?"

I made a face at her. "I never got the chance. Because a certain gorgeous blond I know came in and sat down beside me. Jack spent the rest of the hour whispering to her and forgot about every other girl in the room. Sound familiar?"

She giggled. "Come on, that was nothing. You didn't really have anything going with him."

"So? What about Ronnie Haskins?"

This time she looked slightly guilty. "Oh, that."

"Yes, that. Ronnie actually asked me out."

"You weren't *serious* about him," Megan argued, bending over so that her long hair veiled her face.

"Who's talking serious? The guy asked me out, Megan. In the tenth grade, that's serious enough. We had a real, live date. And when he came to pick me up, who just happened to come wandering across the street?"

Megan bit her lip. "I didn't mean—"

"Don't give me that bull. You'd probably been watching for him to drive up!" I glared at Megan now. "And then you smiled at him and blinked those long lashes, and he invited you to go to the game with us. My first real date! And you crashed it."

"It was his idea. He didn't have to ask me," she murmured.

"Ha! Do flies have any choice when they're caught in a spider's web? Ronnie never looked at me again. He spent the rest of the fall chasing after *you*, and you didn't even want him!"

"He had buck teeth."

I sighed. "You can be a real witch sometimes, Megan. Why do you do it?"

Megan shook her head, hugging her pillow to her chest. "I guess just to prove that I can make a boy like me. Why do you put up with me, Lacey?"

"I don't know," I grumbled. "Crazy, I guess."

She didn't try to argue, just hugged the pillow a little tighter.

"Of course," I relented, "I could mention the time you took all the blame for the broken window."

"You were the prize pupil." Megan shrugged. "You would have lost your honor pin. Me, what did it matter?"

"So you took two weeks' detention, and never told."

"Hey, it was the fifth grade. I was dumb, right?"

I tossed the other pillow at her. I could never stay angry at Megan. "Still are."

A sharp ring interrupted her indignant answer. Megan dived for the phone beside her bed.

"Daddy? I'm so glad you called! Will you be home tonight?"

I picked up a magazine and tried to concentrate on the bright-colored pages, but the eagerness in Megan's tone was hard to ignore.

"But you said—" Megan's voice quivered.

The buzz on the other end resumed.

"Yeah," she said. "See you." She hung up the phone slowly, then finally looked at me.

"He's at Red River; he won't be home until tomorrow afternoon."

Why hadn't Stan Willowby driven on in? Megan followed my thoughts. "He's tired," she explained. "He wanted to get to bed early, then catch up with some paperwork tomorrow."

I tried to look as if I believed that most grown men went to bed at eight in the evening. Especially on a Saturday.

We were both silent, then Megan sat up straighter, with the eager look on her face that I always dreaded. Megan had an idea.

"We could be there in an hour, Lacey. He's at the White Horse Inn. We could surprise him—"

"That's stupid. He'll probably be asleep by the time we got there. I don't want to walk in on your father out of the blue."

"Don't be such a spoilsport," Megan complained. "I'll just say hello; how could he mind that? Then we'll take a swim in the indoor pool they have and drive back. We can do it by midnight, easy."

"No way," I told her. "Count me out."

The light in Megan's eyes faded. "But, Lacey," she begged. "I know what it is. Today was his anniversary, would have been, I mean, if he were still married to my mother. That's why he didn't want to be home tonight. He's probably feeling depressed. It would cheer him up, knowing that I—that somebody cares."

That didn't sound much like Stan Willowby to me.

"It's still not a good idea," I said firmly. "I'm going home. If you're smart, you'll stay right here."

Her pleading look didn't stop me. I walked down the stairs and let myself out without seeing the housekeeper, though I heard the blare of a television set. When I crossed the street, our car wasn't in the carport. My parents must have gone to a movie. But when I walked in the back door, I saw someone in the living room.

Mother sat with her back to me, a pile of books on the desk in front of her. She didn't raise her head.

I didn't speak, trying to sort out a sudden rush of emotion. Dad had gone out alone. He never did that. Were they still fighting? Had things gotten worse?

Almost without realizing it, I found myself back outside the house. I didn't want to stay home, not tonight.

Back across the road, I discovered Megan behind the wheel of the red sports car. She grinned broadly. "I knew you wouldn't let me down."

She turned the red car toward the highway. As I reached for my seat belt, I glanced over my shoulder once more at our empty carport. Tonight, just like Megan, I was running away.

Megan turned the radio up loud and hummed along with the songs. We seemed all alone on the dark highway. Spidery outlines of trees flickered beside the road, and an occasional house zipped by.

"Megan?" I asked suddenly. "Do you remember your mother?"

I didn't expect her to answer. But after a long moment Megan shook her head. "Not much. She was blond, I think. Very pretty."

Like you, I thought. Had the woman who'd left Rockford and her infant daughter, never to return, possessed the same elusive beauty, the same restless energy?

"My dad threw away all my mother's photographs after she left. I used to cut out magazine pictures of pretty blonds," Megan said quietly. "Wondering if one of them looked like my mother."

"That's rough."

"Maybe. But he had reason." Megan frowned into the darkness.

We entered the outskirts of the small town. I began to get nervous. The idea of walking into a motel and knocking on a strange door didn't appeal to me, especially when Stan Willowby was behind the door.

"Megan, are you sure this is such a good idea? We could still forget the whole thing."

She hesitated, but turned away so that I couldn't see her face. "What are you worried about? It's just my dad, right?"

We parked in the motel lot; the motel was large, with an impressive facade that boasted long white columns.

"Do you know what room he's in?"

She didn't answer, but strode purposefully toward the rear wing of the motel. I followed more slowly. I recognized Stan Willowby's big Cadillac as we neared the end of the building.

"Megan," I called. "Wait a minute."

She didn't listen. The door to the last room was firmly shut. Instead of knocking, she headed around the end of the building.

I followed, my sense of foreboding even stronger. The sliding glass doors that led to a small patio were open a crack, and we could hear voices.

Oh, lord, I thought, *he's not alone.* Surely now Megan would back off; instead she headed straight for the motel room. I stopped, but the line of tension in Megan's back, when she halted abruptly at the glass doors, drew me forward again.

A radio played in the background, not soft romantic music but raucous country, interspersed with used-car commercials. The room smelt of cheap perfume and liquor. Stan Willowby lay atop the sheets, wearing only his shorts, a cigarette in his hand, his head thrown back as he stared at the ceiling. Tangled in the sheets by his side was a woman—a girl, a blond girl hardly older than Megan.

Beside me I heard Megan draw a deep, labored breath. I reached for her, thinking she might faint.

Instead she lunged forward, shoving the glass door open with such force that the metal frame rattled. The girl in the bed sat up, pulling the sheet up to cover her breasts, her eyes wide above smeared mascara.

"Who are you?" she gasped. "Stan!"

"What the—?" Stan Willowby started up, then reached for his trousers. Ignoring him, Megan threw herself at the girl on the bed, arms outstretched, murder in her face.

The girl shrieked. I tried to grab Megan.

A whirlwind of fury, she scratched me twice as I tried to pull her back. The girl slid down behind the bed, pulling the sheets with her, still screaming.

Stan Willowby, his trousers half-belted, swore briskly. He lunged around the bed to grab Megan. They struggled for a moment —the tall, slim teenager and her brawny, good-looking father. When he finally brought her arms down to her sides, she spat a few words at him that shocked even me.

Stan Willowby slapped her. The sharp sound of the blow made me gasp. The girl on the floor stopped screaming and stared at them both. Megan was silent, too, a trace of blood staining her lips.

"You're dirt," she told him, her voice ragged. "I hate you!"

"Who are you to judge?" His voice was

harsh with more than liquor, more even than anger.

"She looks like me," Megan whispered, anguish in her voice.

"She looks like your mother," Willowby said.

Megan sagged. I thought she would fall. Her father released her, turning away without waiting to see if she stayed erect. I stepped closer, throwing the man an anxious glance, but he reached for another cigarette, ignoring us both.

"Megan, come on," I begged.

Megan appeared stunned; all the fight had gone out of her. When I took her arm, she followed me out the patio door.

I took the keys from her purse; Megan hardly seemed to notice. When we reached the car, I pushed her into the passenger seat and slammed the door, then slid behind the wheel. When I turned the key, the engine whined as I struggled with the unfamiliar controls. Then I had it in gear, and we pulled out of the parking lot almost as quickly as we'd arrived. The drive home seemed longer than it had coming.

Megan was silent a long time. When she

finally spoke, the wind whistling outside the car and the hum of tires against pavement almost obscured her words.

"Why can't anyone love me?" she said.

CHAPTER

EIGHT

I parked the red convertible in its usual spot behind the Willowby house. "Megan, spend the night at my house, please?"

Megan shook her head. Her face still looked gray and old.

"Do you want me to come up with you?" I offered, afraid of the blank look in her eyes.

She shook her head. "I'd rather be alone."

"You won't do anything stupid?"

Slamming the car door, Megan stretched

her lips into a mocking smile. "What for? It's not like it's anything new—nobody wanting me."

She went inside, slamming the door behind her, and I walked home very slowly.

Our car was back in the carport; Dad must be home. It was too dark to see my watch. I wondered if I was in trouble.

But when I let myself in the back door, a light shone in the front. I peeked into the living room. Mother had closed her books and sat now with a newspaper in her lap.

"I'm home," I said.

"Oh, hello, Lacey." So much for the lecture.

"Where did Dad go?"

"To the poker game at the fire station."

"You don't mind?"

She smiled slightly. "No. He needs some time to himself."

"Do you think it's really worth it?" I remembered all the years of harmony, Mother at home and Dad contented. "This class, I mean. Is it worth all the trouble?"

"It's more than the class, Lacey. But, yes, I think it is."

I bit my lip. How could she sound so calm, so resolute?

"You really want to do this? It means that much to you?"

Mother folded the newspaper. "Yes, it does. Don't you dream about going to medical school, becoming a doctor? You used to tie a white apron around your shoulders and line up all your dolls and teddy bears. 'Time to take your medicine,' you'd tell them." She laughed.

"Sounds silly, doesn't it?" I grinned reluctantly.

"Not at all. Some people know what they want early on, that's all. At your age, I only thought about getting married and having babies."

Mother frowned, and I wondered if she was thinking of the babies she'd lost.

Trying to distract her, I said quickly, "But I want that, too. I want to have a husband and children. I even want to stay home with my babies. I don't want to give those first years away to someone else."

She waited, but when I didn't go on, Mother said, "That sounds fine."

"Do you think I can manage it all?" I asked, suddenly scared.

She reached up to take my hand and pressed it gently. "Everything has a time.

When your father was getting his agency off the ground, I typed his letters and took him tuna sandwiches when he worked late. Then I spent years trying to have a family. Now his business is secure, and you're almost grown. It's time to do something for *me*. Even if it means I have to make some waves." She sighed.

I gave her a quick hug. "You'll do great, I know you will. But do you think Dad will ever come around?"

"I think so," she told me, her tone level. But a wrinkle creased her brow, and I could see the worry in her eyes.

I said good night and went upstairs, and had confused dreams of Kit and Megan and Stan Willowby and my parents until dawn.

Sunday morning I slept late and didn't go to church, and no one even scolded me. I couldn't depend on anything, anymore. I felt as if my world had tilted, and everything around me was sliding toward the edge.

Lying in bed, I watched the sunlight make patterns of light and shadow on the white curtains. I picked up my locket from the bedside table, looking at the inscription for the thousandth time.

Why hadn't Kit put "love" on the little gold heart? What was he afraid of? Had I read too much into his kindness, his loyalty? Just because we'd planned our college schedules together, did that really mean he saw me as part of his future? Maybe I'd jumped ahead too far.

After breakfast I called Kit. "What are you doing?"

"I've got a government report to finish; it's due tomorrow."

Rats, I thought.

Kit asked, "What's wrong?"

"Nothing," I said. "Everything. Want to take a drive after dinner?"

"Sure."

When I hung up the phone, Mother called me to fold clothes. I went without protest, but my thoughts were far away. Later, when Kit pulled into the drive, I ran out to the car.

"What's up?" Kit asked.

I couldn't talk about Megan, not yet. "My mother and father are still barely speaking," I told him. "I'm sick to death of dinners where the only words spoken are,

'Pass the gravy, please,' and 'May I have the pepper?' "

Kit laughed. Some of the tension inside me eased. "Your parents are great people, Lacey. They'll work it out."

"I wish they'd hurry it up." I took a deep breath. "And then there's Megan."

I told him about the disastrous surprise visit last night. "I think most of the crazy things Megan has done in her life—running away when she was thirteen, trying to hitchhike to the Coast last summer—have just been to make her father pay some attention to her."

Kit looked thoughtful. "Did it work?"

"He did bring her back the first time. Last summer he just called the highway patrol to pick her up. But she's tried almost everything, and she's asked me to go along with her almost every time."

"*Do* you go along every time?"

"Of course not." I thought about it for a moment. "I didn't run away, either time."

Kit laughed. After a minute, I did, too.

"Kit?"

"What?"

I glanced at his unruly hair, brightened by the early evening sun, his kind, intelligent eyes, then turned back to stare at the rip in the dashboard.

"Don't you care for me anymore?" I spoke so softly I wasn't sure he heard.

He sighed and leaned forward, resting his forehead against the steering wheel. "You know I do."

"How much?"

"Come on, Lacey—"

"I mean it. Where are we going, the two of us?"

"To college." He sat upright again, sounding firm.

"That's not what I meant."

"That's enough for now."

"Why? What's wrong with thinking ahead?"

"Lacey, leave it!" Kit, who never raised his voice, sounded genuinely angry. His blue eyes were hard.

I drew back to the far edge of the seat. "Don't I have the right to know how you feel?"

"For Pete's sake, Lacey! If you don't know by now—" He still sounded exasperated, but the hard edge in his voice had eased.

I saw the old, familiar Kit again and

blinked in relief. He must have read my face, because he reached out and put his arm around my shoulders, pulling me closer.

I laid my head against his chest, listening to the muffled sound of his heartbeat, so regular and reassuring.

When I lifted my face, Kit kissed me, softly at first, then long and hard. My heart jumped. I kissed him back. All my pent-up worry merged with a new depth of need.

He pulled away. I reached for him, pulled him gently back. He touched my lips for a moment, then straightened again.

"Lacey, you know we agreed—"

"I don't care!" I wanted Kit to kiss me, hold me. I wanted—more than I had the nerve to say.

"You're being stupid." Kit's voice had lost its cool control. "Don't do this, Lacey."

"Why not?" The black anger inside me boiled over; I felt as if I'd been rejected one time too many. "Why do I always have to be good little Lacey? Megan does what she wants, and she's got plenty of boys to do it with. Maybe I should start taking lessons from her!"

"Lacey!"

"Megan always—"

"Forget Megan! If it were *Megan* I wanted, I could have her."

I jerked as if he'd hit me. "Sure of yourself, aren't you?"

We glared at each other inside the darkened car.

"Why not? Every other boy in town has."

"I hate you!" I cried. Then I jumped out blindly, slammed the door hard, and ran for home.

CHAPTER
NINE

I spent a restless night, waking early, re-sisting the urge to call Kit.

"I didn't mean it," I wanted to tell him. But I couldn't. If he cared, he would be the one to call. Wouldn't he?

I climbed out of bed and dressed. I picked up my locket and read the inscription again. It had been almost enough, when I was sure that Kit loved me. But now—

I hung the narrow chain around my neck and went down to breakfast, but I didn't have any appetite. I poured a bowl of cereal, took a few bites, then decided that I couldn't wait any longer. When Mother left the kitchen, I grabbed the phone and dialed Kit's number. His little sister answered.

"Is Kit there?"

"He's already left for school."

I hoped I could talk to him before classes, but of all mornings, Megan was late. By the time we got to school, the first bell had rung. We ran to class and even then I was late. If I hadn't been so full of my own worries, I might have noticed how morose and silent Megan was, but I couldn't think of anything except Kit.

I sat through my classes like a zombie, ignoring the others, even Megan and John Paul and the rest of my group as they rehearsed the *Othello* skit. I hurried to the cafeteria at lunchtime, hoping Kit would be waiting in the usual spot. He wasn't there. I stood in the back of the room and waited, but there was no sign of him. He didn't want to see me.

The rest of the day seemed blurred. I sat in the back of my classes and ignored the droning voices of the teachers, the chatter of the other kids.

"What's wrong with you?" Megan demanded as we drove home.

"Nothing." I glanced at her face—she didn't look exactly blissful herself—and asked cautiously, "Did your dad come home?"

She didn't answer for a moment, and her lips tightened. Then she shook her head. "No. He called Mrs. Frog yesterday. Said he won't be home for a couple of weeks—till he cools off, he said. He's still too mad to talk to me now."

"Rough," I murmured, afraid to say more.

Megan stared at the road ahead, her hands gripping the wheel so hard her knuckles whitened. We finished the drive in silence.

When I walked into the kitchen, Mother was sifting flour, a dab of it on her nose. She looked like the old, familiar mother I had grown up with, not the one suddenly set on striking out into new territory.

"What do you do when you've had a really serious disagreement with someone you care about?" I asked.

She raised her head, but didn't ask any of the questions I dreaded. Instead she bent over the dough she was mixing in the big bowl. "If you care enough about one another, you can usually find some kind of compromise." She brushed back a strand of hair, streaking flour across her cheek now. "Usually."

"Why does being in love cause so many problems?" I complained. "I thought love was supposed to make you happy."

Mother seemed lost in thought. "Sometimes it does . . . but you can give too much of yourself away when you love. And there's no happiness in that."

What did that mean? From the corner of my eye, I saw a flicker of movement beyond the doorway. Dad stood just outside the kitchen. He didn't move, and I was too intent on Mother's words to wonder about him.

"I thought love meant thinking about the other person," I persisted.

"It does," Mother agreed. "But the other person has to think about you, too. Love can't be one-sided."

She pounded her dough. Dad had already walked away. I wandered upstairs and sat

120

down on my bed for a moment, then jumped up as if something had bitten me. I dialed the familiar number and again got Kit's little sister.

"Is Kit home?"

"That you again, Lacey? He's at work."

Was he still avoiding me? I told myself not to be silly, Kit worked every day after school.

It wasn't that far to the drugstore. Grabbing my jacket, I walked toward the center of town. The afternoon was bright and sunny, but the air was cool. I turned up the collar of my jacket, wishing I'd brought a scarf. But the cold wind made me walk faster, and it wasn't long before I came to Main Street. Rockford's one drugstore was a small, neat brick building. I saw Kit through the front window, but he had his back to me. I watched him for a moment, feeling a lump in my throat and shivering from more than the cold breeze.

A bell jangled as I swung the door open. A customer stood in the back of the store talking to Mr. Patton. Alone in the front, Kit stacked boxes of tissue on a shelf.

"Hi."

Kit glanced up, then back to the carton

he was emptying. He had a closed look on his face that I'd never seen before. My throat ached. I tried not to let my voice wobble.

"I didn't mean it, Kit."

For a moment he still refused to look at me. I felt a stab of desolation. Was he so angry he wouldn't even listen?

He placed the last box on the shelf. "I know."

I felt more confused than ever. If he understood how much I cared for him, how could he look so distant?

"Kit, it's just that I—I love you. I love you so much that I want to be close to you."

I had said it. I knew my face was flushed. I studied the design of the worn flooring, afraid that Kit would be frightened by the one word he had so studiously avoided.

"I know, Lacey."

It was my turn to be angry. I glared at him. "If you know, why did you pull away from me like that?"

"Because love is dangerous, Lacey."

"What are you talking about?"

Kit took a deep breath. He looked toward the back of the store and called, "I'm going to take a break, Mr. Patton. Five minutes, okay?"

When his employer didn't object, Kit took me by the arm and steered me to the door. Outside, the cool air made me gulp. Kit let go of my arm as the door shut behind us.

"Now listen," he said. "She doesn't want anybody to know, yet, but if I can't tell *you*—"

"Tell me what?"

"It's Carla."

He hesitated. A vivid memory of his sister's face as I had last seen it—her eyes swollen and red—flashed into my mind.

"She and her husband have split up, Lacey. They'll probably get a divorce. She dropped out of school to marry him, because of the baby. Now she's eighteen, no diploma, a baby to support. What's she going to do?"

I didn't know what to say. His face held both worry and frustration, and his voice was hard.

"I'm not risking *our* future, yours and mine. What if you got pregnant? You want to go through an abortion?"

I drew back instinctively. "I couldn't! We'd use protection—we'd be careful."

"That's what Carla thought," Kit said, his voice grim. "No birth control works all the time. We're not taking that chance. We have plans—both of us. We're going to college, Lacey. You're going to do all the things you've dreamed about. I won't have you giving up your ambitions, not for me."

Even in the chilly air, he had drops of sweat on his forehead.

"I understand," I told him. "I'm sorry I tried to push you. It's okay. We won't do anything. I don't care about sex. You're going to college; I'm going to college. We won't blow it. But I care about you. I *love* you, Kit. Is that so bad?"

"Love gets in the way, Lacey. We have too far to go to make any promises now."

"I didn't ask for a promise." I could feel my face flush. "I didn't ask for anything. I said we would cool it. What are you afraid of?"

"You're not Megan." Kit stared at me, his expression twisted. "Loyalty is your middle name, Lacey. You can't take love lightly. I don't think I'm ready."

"What?" I felt as if the ground had

dropped suddenly beneath me, like an elevator going too fast. My stomach wobbled.

"It's not you," Kit said. "Can't you understand? Ever since my dad died, I've had to worry about someone else—my mom, my sisters. Carla's marriage breaking up is just the last straw. I have to get this scholarship, just to get to college, then it's making the grades, making enough money. I don't think I can take any more pressure."

"I wasn't trying to pressure you." My voice sounded stiff, even to me.

"I know."

The sharp sound of rapping made us both jump.

"Kit?" Inside the store, Mr. Patton waved from behind the glass. "I need a hand."

"Coming." To me Kit said, "I have to go. Are you okay?"

"I'm fine."

He opened the door, making the bell tinkle again, and went inside. I began to walk slowly toward home. The cold wind numbed my face, but there was a bigger numbness inside me. I wanted to cry, but this was too big for tears. I loved Kit, to the depths of my soul. And Kit wasn't ready to love me.

Dad was sitting in the den when I got home, reading the paper. I could hear my mother moving around in the kitchen, and it occurred to me that this was how it had always been—Mother at home, waiting for him. Maybe it was hard to change habits that had lasted for years.

"If you care enough about someone, you can work out disagreements, can't you?" I asked Dad.

For a moment I didn't think he'd heard. His hand moved slightly as he lowered the paper.

"Can't you?" I repeated.

"Lacey, don't you have homework to do?"

Men! I thought. They never said what you wanted them to.

CHAPTER

TEN

Mrs. Williams had scheduled our Shake-speare skits for Tuesday. I felt as jittery as a kitten, even though we had rehearsed for a week. Megan seemed strangely excited. Her blue eyes glittered, and her cheeks were pink with suppressed emotion.

It didn't help my nerves when Mrs. Williams announced that we were moving down to the library because she had invited two other English classes to watch. They filed in and took seats along the back wall, while we cleared the front of the room to make enough space for our performances.

There were four skits in all. The first three were pretty bad. At least the other groups had had the foresight to choose comedies. Then it was time for our group. My knees wobbled as I walked in front of the audience to make my introduction. "*Othello*, a tragedy by William Shakespeare." I tried to keep my voice from shaking. "The play concerns the noble Moorish general, Othello; his virtuous bride, Desdemona; and the treacherous Iago. . . ."

I scanned the crowd of students, wishing Kit were there. Buddy sat in the back of the room, looking half-asleep. A couple of girls giggled behind their hands.

Megan had put together a good skit; Ron and David had brief roles as the wicked Iago and Cassio, the lieutenant whom Othello mistakenly believes to be his wife's lover. Sue Ann made a brief appearance as Desdemona's serving woman.

But John Paul and Megan dominated the scene of Othello and his wife in their last climactic encounter. John Paul was not particularly gifted as an actor, though he spoke his lines clearly and gravely. But his tall, well-built body lent dignity to his portrayal of the noble general, and I forgot this was only a brief student sketch and caught a glimpse of the real tragedy.

And Megan—Megan was breathtaking. She spoke her part with such fervor that a prickling of tears burned behind my lids as she, the falsely accused bride, tried to make her beloved husband believe her innocence. Her speech quieted the restless students, now genuinely absorbed.

There was anguish in Megan's face when Othello shouted, "Think of thy sins!"

Megan replied, "They are loves I bear to you."

Then John Paul gripped her neck, his big hands dark against Megan's fair skin. Megan's head was thrown back, her eyes bright and beseeching, while her long pale hair fell over his fingers like a lover's caress.

When the skit ended, there was a moment of silence. Then applause exploded, and Mrs. Williams clapped harder than anyone.

A crowd of students rushed to praise them. John Paul looked embarrassed and got out of the circle of admirers as quickly as possible. Megan, caught in the crowd, looked distracted.

I waited till the group began to drift away, then walked over.

"Meryl Streep, I presume?"

"Cut it out."

"You were good," I told her. "Seriously."

"Thanks."

The lunch bell rang and we turned toward the door. A large, broad figure stepped in front of us. Buddy.

He didn't appear to come bearing compliments. A frown twisted his face, and lines of tension creased his wide forehead.

Megan gave him a blank stare; she had ignored him since the night of the party. When she paused, as if welcoming another confrontation, I said, "See you later, Megan." At that moment I couldn't play mother hen.

"Right."

I walked toward the cafeteria to find Kit. As I stopped at my locker, I realized I was glad that Kit hadn't seen Megan playing her part with such eloquent beauty.

I leaned a moment against the cool metal door, wondering if I would ever get over my feelings of inadequacy when it came to Megan. How could I care so much for her and almost hate her at the same time?

Kit waited in the usual place. "Hi," he said, with something close to his normal smile.

"Hi yourself," I replied.

We walked into the lunchroom, and I forgot about everyone's problems but my own.

I met Megan in the parking lot after school. "Did Buddy give you a hard time?"

"That clown? Nothing I can't handle."

"What'd he want?" I opened the door and slipped into the car beside her.

"Still trying to tell me what to do." Megan's smile held a hint of mystery as she backed the car out of its parking space. Sunlight glinted off her pale hair, and the curve of her cheek as she glanced over her shoulder was smooth and cleanly sculpted.

No wonder Buddy didn't want to give her up.

"Does he think you're still going out with Tim?"

"Who?" Megan said. "Oh, Tim. I don't think so."

"Then who's Buddy jealous of now?" I asked. And then I took a risk. "John Paul?"

Megan laughed, and I laughed, too, nervously. She hadn't answered my question.

It turned out I didn't have to wait much longer for an answer. In trig class two days later, Mary Lou Reynolds tapped me on the shoulder as I glanced over my homework.

"Did you figure out the last problem?" I asked.

Mary Lou wasn't interested in math. "Lacey, honey," she told me, "I feel so sorry for you."

I sat up straighter, my mind filled with horrible speculations. "What do you mean?" My voice was sharper than I had intended it to be.

Mary Lou looked pleased. "I know how hard you've worked, trying to keep that girl out of trouble—" Mary Lou sounded like an echo of her mother, sweet and infinitely treacherous.

"What are you talking about?" I felt like a trout being dangled on the hook.

"Megan, of course," Mary Lou drawled.

"I know how loyal you are to her, but Megan and John Paul—I mean, really!"

"It was only a skit. They were acting!" I protested, maybe too strongly.

"Were they? I'm sure you know all about it." Mary Lou lowered her lids slightly, her eyes gleaming with malice. "She won't get away with it this time, Lacey. She's pushed the limits before, but this is *too much.*"

The teacher rapped on his desk for attention, and Mary Lou fell silent, leaving me with a cold feeling of apprehension.

Was Mary Lou just spreading one of her usual nasty rumors?

It didn't help that in study hall I walked in on a small group of girls, heads together, whispering furiously. When they saw me, they stopped abruptly. I sat down at my desk, biting my lip.

At the end of the day I hurried to the parking lot, determined to get to the bottom of this.

"Do you know what half the school's talking about?" I demanded.

"What?" Megan unlocked the convertible, leaning on the plastic top.

"Mary Lou seems to think you're

seriously interested in John Paul. Is she just being as cross-eyed as usual, or have you pulled something new?"

Megan turned the key in the ignition. "So, maybe she's right."

My mind went blank. It was like seeing the world upside down. I spoke very carefully.

"Are you serious? Just because of the skit? Don't get carried away with a fantasy, Megan."

"It's not a fantasy. And it's not just the skit. I walked to class with John Paul this morning. And you know how these kids gossip." Megan smiled.

I shut my eyes while the air whistled past the half-open window. Hadn't I seen this coming? Hadn't I had a suspicion, and hadn't I tried to ignore it?

"You like John Paul?" I asked, trying to rearrange my whole inner vision.

"Don't you?" She slowed for a red light.

"Of course." My voice was hoarse; I had to clear my throat. "Everyone likes John Paul; he's easygoing and polite, not to mention being the star of the basketball team. Everybody likes a winner—especially you."

Megan's smile died. "Low blow, Lacey."

"That's why you've been to every basketball game," I continued, not apologizing. "That's why you were hanging around Tim—just for the excuse to be with the team. You were never really interested in Tim, were you, Megan? You just wanted to be near John Paul, and even you had to work up to that one."

She smiled a Cheshire-cat smile.

"Don't be so smug," I yelled. "You can't do it, Megan."

"Why not?"

"Because, you moron, he's *black*."

The word was out. The silence inside the car felt very heavy. Megan turned into our street and slowed the convertible. At my driveway she turned to stare at me.

"I didn't expect that. From everyone else, maybe, but not from you."

"Megan—"

"I didn't think you'd be like all the rest."

"Megan, it's not prejudice—at least—" The anxiety inside me was too strong for soul-searching. "At least I don't think it is. But you've got to use some common sense. This isn't New York or Los Angeles. It's not even Atlanta. This is Rockford,

Mississippi, population three thousand four hundred and sixty-two."

"Sixty-four," Megan murmured. "Mrs. Roderick had twins last week."

"Megan! Think about what you're doing."

"That sort of thinking is out-of-date." Megan waved her free hand airily. "We're not living in the Dark Ages."

"Megan, the kids at school—"

"I don't care!" Her voice rose. "I don't care what they say—all the *nice* girls in this rotten town. They've never forgotten my mother's disgrace—running off with a two-bit shoe salesman. Why should they expect any less from me?"

Her face was white with patches of red, and her eyes glittered.

"You're the one who can't forget, Megan," I told her. "I don't know what you're trying to prove. But whatever it is you're planning to do, *don't*."

"Why not?" Megan taunted. "What else can they do to me? You're the only *nice* girl in town who speaks to me now."

"What do you think your father will say?"

Her eyes sparkled, and a new excitement

made her purse her lips. "He'll say I'm just like my mother, I guess."

It doesn't matter what he says, I thought, *as long as he notices. That's all Megan wants.*

"You're willing to be talked about by half the town?"

"That's right! I don't care."

"You've forgotten one thing," I told her, slamming the car door. "Maybe John Paul does."

CHAPTER
ELEVEN

From that time on I felt like a hamster on a miniature treadmill. Trying to keep Megan under constant observation when we had only one class together wasn't easy. But fortunately, senior English was the only class either she or I shared with John Paul, and Rockford High wasn't the biggest school in the world.

"Late again?" Mrs. Williams asked, her voice sharp, as I slipped inside the classroom Wednesday.

"Sorry, I—I forgot my notebook," I stammered.

I was running out of excuses. I was spending all my breaks cruising the halls, trying to keep my eye on Megan.

Megan stayed on the move, trying to capture John Paul's attention. But he seemed to be avoiding her, which gave me my one spark of hope.

He wasn't the only one. Until her bitter comments in the car that afternoon when I'd confronted her with the rumors, I'd almost forgotten how much of a pariah Megan had become. Wednesday afternoon a group of girls gossiping in a doorway fell silent at her approach. Megan, aware of their hostile glances, tossed her long hair in apparent disdain. But she slammed the locker door with unusual force.

"Take it easy," I murmured. "I thought you didn't care what people said about you."

Megan stretched her lips into a furious grin. "Of course not."

But she walked rapidly toward her next class, her back stiff and her shoulders set.

My skin wasn't so thick. Susan Mason took me aside that afternoon in government. "Lacey, what's wrong with you? You've been acting strangely all week."

"What are you talking about?"

"I don't know why you stand up for Megan," she insisted. "The girl has no sense, and with that family! Mary Lou's talking about you. She thinks you've been hanging around Megan so long it's beginning to rub off."

"Really?" Anger made me blunt. "Does she believe that thinking for yourself is like face powder? Tell her not to get too close."

Susan shook her head. "I just wanted you to know what people are saying. For your own good."

"Don't do me any favors."

She frowned and went back to her desk.

I sat down and flipped through my textbook, feeling very much alone. How did Megan stand it?

I wanted to talk to Kit about it all, but I knew that Megan was a sensitive subject. He'd just get mad again. Besides, when I was with Kit, I had other problems on my mind. Like him and me.

On Thursday I discovered Megan and John Paul together at the end of the hallway. Megan, her head thrown back to meet his eyes, talked rapidly. The expres-

sion on her face was not one of artful se-
duction; it was more like wistful appeal. I
remembered Kit's having compared her to
a confused puppy hoping for a kind word,
ready either to lick or bite an outstretched
hand.

I stared at John Paul, afraid he would ex-
hibit the bemused and blissful confusion
that Megan usually evoked in any boy she
chose to charm. I still saw glimpses of it in
Buddy, though it had been almost completely replaced by bitter anger. Instead,
John Paul's face appeared carefully blank.

I hurried up to them, aware that everyone else in the hall, black or white, threw
covert glances toward the pair. None of the
glances were friendly.

"Hi, Megan," I said brightly. "Sorry I'm
late."

The glance she gave me was savage, but I
linked arms with her and chatted away
cheerfully and idiotically until John Paul
glanced at his watch.

"Time for class," he murmured, turning
toward the other end of the hall.

When he'd walked out of earshot, Megan
hissed at me. "Leave me alone, Lacey."

She pushed my arm away, her voice tight with anger.

"Don't you remember what happened to Marietta Kelsey?"

"Who?"

"The woman who used to run the beer hall outside of town. She took up with a black salesman from Birmingham."

"So?" Megan sounded bored.

"Not only did she lose most of her customers, someone burned down her place."

"That was years ago. Anyhow, I heard it was faulty wiring."

"Sure. She got threatening phone calls, Megan. The woman had to leave town."

"That's stupid."

"I know it's stupid. But too many people in Rockford just don't believe in interracial romances. And some of those people do more than talk!"

Her lower lip jutted out, and her tone remained stubborn. "I don't let other people tell me how to run my life."

I wanted to shake her. "I just want to keep you in one piece—and John Paul, too. Being a bodyguard is hard work, you moron, and you don't even appreciate my efforts."

Megan rolled her eyes. "You're making a big deal out of nothing. Just relax, okay?"

"I wish I could. Let's get to class."

There was worse to come.

Friday I went to English class as usual, thinking that this hour was safe, at least. John Paul would be in class, and therefore, so would Megan. But Megan wasn't at her desk.

Puzzled, I checked the other side of the room. John Paul was missing, too. I sat up straighter, feeling my pulse quicken. Now what?

"Where's John Paul?" I whispered to the girl behind me.

"I heard the basketball team's having a secret meeting in the locker room. They want to plan a surprise gift for the head coach."

I noticed that several other boys on the team were missing, too. But that didn't account for Megan. What was she up to?

The second bell hadn't rung, though it would any second.

"Tell Mrs. Williams I've gone to the rest room," I said.

Megan wasn't at her locker. Feeling a

strong wave of foreboding, I turned toward the gym. The late bell rang, and I started to run, hoping I wouldn't encounter a teacher. I made it to the gymnasium unobserved and slipped through the double doors.

At first glance the gym appeared deserted. Yet I knew Megan's disappearance must have something to do with the team meeting. Was she planning to waylay John Paul on the way back to class? Her attempts to get his attention were becoming more and more blatant.

Then a slight movement at the corner of my vision made me stiffen.

Was it Megan? But even Megan would never dare invade the sanctity of the boys' locker room. Then I realized it would be just the kind of outrageous stunt she would most enjoy—shocking the whole school and probably getting herself suspended, just months before graduation.

I hurried toward the end of the gym, paused, took a deep breath, then pushed through the swinging door.

"Megan!" I hissed. "What do you think you're up to?"

Megan had been peeking around the

door, sure enough. She glared back at me. She sat on one of the benches, her feet drawn up beneath her.

"Who are you, my shadow?"

"What are you doing here?" I could distinguish a murmur of voices from behind the closed inner door.

"I wanted to see John Paul." Megan's blue eyes dared me to criticize.

"A nice, private little meeting," I snapped. "In the middle of the whole basketball team? You're crazy in the head, Megan Willowby. You'll be the joke of the entire school."

"Shut your mouth!"

"Do you think John Paul will be happy? They'll be laughing at him, too." I tried to keep my voice low, afraid we would be heard past the closed door, but my voice wobbled up and down like an accordion. "Megan, don't you ever *think* about what you're doing?"

"Why should I?" Megan demanded. "You're always there telling me what to do. Don't you think we're past the mother hen–little chick business?" She tossed her long hair in the familiar gesture. "Why don't you just leave me alone?"

"They're going to laugh at you, Megan," I told her, adding in desperation, "John Paul will laugh at you."

"He will not!" Megan shouted, jumping to her feet. "You take that back!"

The inner door opened, and a crowd of boys spilled into the room, their eyes big with curiosity and surprise. Behind them—the assistant coach. Coach Jenkins appeared so angry that he opened and shut his mouth several times before he spoke.

I froze.

"*What* are you two doing here?" Coach Jenkins controlled his voice with an effort, but a vein in his throat throbbed visibly.

I stared at the pulsing vein in fascination, waiting for Megan to come up with one of her usual easy excuses. But she remained silent.

The coach turned to me.

"I—we—it was a dare," I blurted.

"A dare?" The coach spat. "Two seniors taking a dare? Dares are for children."

Most of the boys were grinning, and a few began to chuckle. Only John Paul remained grave. He didn't say a word. After one quick glance, I didn't look at him again.

"If I take you to the office, you'll be suspended for a week," the coach said.

What would my mother say?

The warm, still air inside the locker room felt heavy with the stale smell of unwashed socks and soured towels. I felt a sudden stab of nausea, and the room whirled.

"Catch her," the coach said from far away.

Someone grabbed my arm. Megan held me upright, and I clung to her, while the room settled back into place.

"Okay, both of you get out of here," Coach Jenkins said. "If I ever see you two within twenty yards of this room, I'll tan your hides myself and feed them to the mosquitoes."

"Yes, sir," I said. Megan followed me through the doorway, and I could feel the stares of the boys hard on my back until the door swung shut behind us.

The cooler air of the gym felt as welcome as a dash of cold water. My stomach calmed.

"Talk about performances," Megan murmured. "You get the Oscar for that one."

"I wasn't faking," I told her indignantly.

148

"But you'd better thank your lucky stars we got out of it so lightly."

"My stars aren't lucky," Megan said. "I thought you knew."

When we got to English class, Mrs. Williams greeted us with a caustic smile. "Nice of you girls to grace us with your presence." She glanced at the clock on the wall. "The fact that the class is half over is, I'm sure, merely an oversight. You two may stay thirty minutes after the bell to make up your work."

Megan swore under her breath.

I just sat and worried about what Kit would say.

Sure enough, when I finally made it to the cafeteria, Kit's expression was tight with annoyance. Megan and I might have been late to lunch, but the basketball team had been on time, and they had wasted no time in spreading the story.

"Lacey, why?" Kit asked, his eyes steely with anger.

I set down my glass of milk—my stomach was still too queasy for food—and settled into the chair beside him. "Megan—"

"It's always Megan!" Kit's voice was loud. "She gets into some mess, and you end up taking the blame. What good does it do?"

"I'm her friend."

"How can you be her friend when all she ever does is get you into trouble?"

"She's like my sister. You of all people should understand that, Kit. Don't you take care of your family? Any time Ellen or Carla needs help, don't you help them? Megan doesn't have anyone but me."

"Lacey, I worry about you."

That was the nicest thing he'd said to me in a week. It made him even harder to resist. I wanted to throw my arms around Kit and promise that I would never follow Megan into another disaster. But the words stuck on my tongue. I couldn't promise what I knew in my heart I couldn't do.

Kit shook his head at my continued silence. "Lacey, don't you think you've done enough for her?"

"I haven't done *anything* yet, nothing that's worked, anyway."

"That's not what I mean. You're not doing Megan any favors."

I swallowed a groan; Megan would agree with that.

"She's not a child anymore, Lacey. She has to pay for her own mistakes. Back off."

I stared down at the mustard stains on the tabletop, unable to meet his eyes. "This is not just another stunt, Kit. She's really freaked out. I can't just turn my back on her, I can't."

Kit stabbed his straw into his milk shake until it crumpled. "And I don't know how much longer I can watch you taking the fallout from Megan's disasters!"

CHAPTER

TWELVE

I half expected Megan to leave without me after school, but she was waiting in the parking lot, her expression sulky. We drove home in silence. Had she heard the snickers that followed us now as the locker-room story spread through the school? I only hoped our unwanted notoriety would fade by Monday.

My family enjoyed another icily polite dinner at home. Mother's eyes seemed sad all the time now, and Dad usually hid behind the paper or pretended to be absorbed in the television screen. Even during dinner he stared at his plate as if he had an abiding interest in his mashed potatoes.

Kit and I had planned to go to the basketball game—Rockford High was still winning, and spirits were high—but I couldn't take any more contact with the ball team, not yet. I wasn't even sure Kit would show up for our date. But he did, only a few minutes late. I ran to let him in.

"Friends?" I asked anxiously, trying to read his expression.

"What else?"

Relieved, I proved it with a quick hug.

We went to a mediocre movie. I rested my head on Kit's shoulder while he struggled to keep up with the plot, and we didn't talk much.

I didn't expect to see Megan that weekend, sure that she would nurse her anger for some time. So I was surprised to hear her voice when I answered the phone Saturday, just before noon.

"Lacey, want to take a ride with me?"

"Where?" I was instantly suspicious.

"I'm going to John Paul's house."

I sat down hard on the kitchen chair,

thankful that Mother was upstairs. "Megan, what good will that do?"

"I want to talk to him." Megan's voice sounded sullen, but I could hear the rock-hard obstinacy underneath. "Just a few minutes without the roof falling; that's all I ask. At school everybody's against us—there's always someone around, and he won't—I mean—"

"And you're asking *me* to go with you?"

"I thought you'd jump at the chance. You haven't left me alone a minute all week."

She's scared, I thought.

Megan must have read my thoughts. "If you don't come, I'll go alone." Her tone hardened. "I thought it might look more casual, you know, if there were two of us."

She's not sure how he feels, I realized. "What about John Paul? He may not *want* to talk to you. Why do you think he avoids you at school?"

"He's not avoiding me," Megan insisted. "It's just—you know, the other kids—"

"Megan, leave him alone. If you *have* to talk to him, call him on the phone."

"I tried that." Her voice was bleak. "His family doesn't have a phone."

"Oh."

"I'm going," she announced. "If you want to come, be here in five minutes."

I grabbed my jacket.

We drove in silence, turning into a side of town I wasn't familiar with, crossing the railroad track and passing the mill. The houses that had been mostly neat and trim had begun to deteriorate. Some were still nicely kept, with small lawns, but others —rentals, I guessed—had paint hanging in strips, and the lawns were only overgrown collections of weeds, with occasional bare spots where small black children played.

"Do you know where he lives?"

"I think so." Megan sounded vague. "But some of these houses don't have numbers."

I had lived in this town all my life and never before driven down this street. The thought jarred me.

We both stared at the houses, searching in vain for markers. A child glanced at us curiously, and a man leaning on a junked car gave us a hard look that made me want to sink down into the seat. Megan slowed the car and rolled down the window.

"Can you tell me where the Waters family lives, please?"

I thought he wasn't going to answer.

"What for?"

"It's church work," Megan said. Megan, who set foot in a church only when my mother insisted.

"Three houses down, that side." He turned away.

The house was small and painfully neat. Beside a struggling patch of grass, flowers had been planted. They looked as if they had been stepped on more than once, but the hope was there.

Megan parked the car in the scattered patch of gravel that passed for a driveway. I thought I saw a movement at the window.

Megan started toward the house. I ran after her.

There was no doorbell. Megan knocked on the wooden door, lightly at first, then more firmly.

The door creaked open, and a small child stared up at us. She had a profusion of spiky black braids and wore faded overalls and a long-sleeved shirt.

Megan flashed her most charming smile. "Is John Paul home? Can I see him?"

The little girl grinned and ducked out of sight.

Megan relaxed, as if she had passed the first hurdle in a difficult race. I chewed on my lip, wondering how many pairs of eyes were watching us.

The door swung open again, and Megan took a slight step forward, only to check herself abruptly.

A large, broad woman stood in the doorway. Her expression was grim, flattening her wide mouth into a hard line. She wiped her hands on the plaid apron that covered her faded house dress. I thought of a biblical phrase, "girding his loins," and understood those words for the first time. This woman was preparing to do battle.

"What you want with John Paul?" she demanded.

Megan seemed taken aback. "I just wanted to talk to him—" she began.

"What business you got with John Paul?" Her hands dry, Mrs. Waters planted her fists firmly on each broad hip and stared down at Megan with immense disdain.

"He's a friend of—" Under the shrewd, appraising stare of John Paul's mother,

Megan faltered. "We have a class together at the high school. I wanted to discuss a project with him."

"You got schoolwork, you talk about it at school," the woman commanded. "Don't come round here."

Megan's face paled. "I just wanted—"

"John Paul's a good boy," Mrs. Waters said, her tone fierce. "He's smart, and he's a good boy. He's the best ball player this town's ever had, and he's going to get himself a scholarship to a fancy college. John Paul's going to make something of himself. He don't need no trouble."

"I don't want to cause any—"

"For John Paul, you're the worst trouble there is!" Mrs. Waters shook one finger at Megan and slammed the door in our faces.

We walked quickly back to the car. Megan was silent as she started the engine, then pulled the car out of the rutted driveway, turning toward home.

The sun shone low in the sky as Megan braked for the four-way stop at the mill road. A yellow pickup truck pulled up to the left of us. I heard a muffled shout. Buddy had spotted Megan.

The gears on his truck grated, then he

jumped out of the cab and ran to the side of the car. Before Megan could touch the accelerator, Buddy jerked open the car door and hauled her bodily into the road.

"Get your hands off me!" Megan shrieked.

Buddy held Megan by the shoulders, throwing her against the side of the car.

"Get my hands off? That wasn't what you said the night of the homecoming dance, Megan. You liked my hands well enough that night. You forget so quick?"

Megan's lips curled in anger. "I think you're despicable," she said, her voice shaking with rage.

"I was okay when I was captain of the football team! More than okay."

"Get lost, Buddy!"

"But football season's over, isn't it? Took me a while to figure out why you were in such a hurry to dump me. Now you're after a new patsy. Who is it, Megan? Who've you been to see, past Mill Road?"

Megan pressed her lips together.

"I didn't know you went visiting in shantytown, Megan. You sunk that low?"

Megan, already pale, now turned white.

"The lowest I ever sunk was when I went out with you!"

Buddy's eyes narrowed, and he drew back a hand.

I threw myself half out the open window. "Buddy, no!"

He seemed to see me for the first time. He lowered his arm slowly, but he still held Megan pinned to the side of the car.

"You're scum, Megan Willowby. Lower than scum. When the boys at school hear about this, no decent guy will look at you, I promise."

Megan kicked him hard in the shin, jerked away, and dived for the car. I slipped back into my seat. We pulled away amid the rattle of flying gravel.

"What's he doing?" Megan gasped, her eyes on the road as she tried to control the wheel.

"He's getting into his truck." I peered through the rear window. "Oh, help."

"What?"

"He's coming after us."

Megan pushed hard against the gas pedal, and the car careened down the narrow road.

"Oh, no!" I yelled.

A freight train chugged its leisurely way across the track ahead. I turned to stare at Buddy's truck, right behind us. "Now what?"

Megan jerked the wheel. The convertible quivered, then resisted a tendency to roll. We slid into a small alley, clipping an overflowing trash can and sending it tumbling against the back wall of a liquor store.

"Did Buddy see us?"

"How could he miss?"

Buddy's truck struck the fallen trash can with a crash, sending it flying once more.

Megan, barred by the freight train from going toward town, turned and headed back the way we had come. I shut my eyes and prayed. When Megan came to the intersection, she turned south, toward farmland and shaggy pines.

Her small car sped ahead, and for the first time I felt thankful for its powerful engine. But the truck was still behind us, always there when I looked over my shoulder.

"He's still coming."

We sped past pasture and fields of cotton and soybeans, lying fallow now, with only

162

straggling reminders of last fall's harvest. Then the road narrowed, with only pines and scrub brush to each side. There were no more houses. I glanced again at the pickup truck still in pursuit, hearing the roar of its engine above the slight whine of the sports car. Where were we heading?

"Megan, this road is a dead end! What are we going to do?"

We hit a deep rut. The car swayed dangerously, bounced once, and kept going.

Buddy's truck, better suited for this rough road, gained on us. The big cab loomed closer. I shut my eyes. When I opened them again, craning my neck toward the back, I shrieked. "Look out!"

The truck came at us like a charging bull. Its fender touched our rear bumper, grazing it, and the whole car shuddered. Megan fought with the wheel and by some miracle kept the car on the road.

I thought of Buddy's clenched fist. The truck was even deadlier. I was afraid to look back, but I had to.

"He's coming!"

Megan jerked the wheel. The world whirled around us. The car rocked, rose briefly to angle over, its weight on two wheels, then somehow righted itself. Megan hit the window, then ricocheted back at me. Our heads met with a painful thud. The seat belt held me back from the dashboard, but the force of the impact made me bite through my bottom lip. I tasted blood.

The car continued to slide, ripping through bushes that scratched at its sides. Somehow we missed the bigger trees.

Buddy didn't.

There was a crash, the crunch of metal meeting a solid tree trunk. Wood splintered as the tree—split by the impact—fell to the ground with a series of hollow thuds, while showers of pine needles rattled on the roof of the truck.

"Wait, Megan," I begged. "See if Buddy's all right."

"Who cares?" She leaned her head against the wheel, trembling.

Buddy crawled out of the cab. He seemed shaken but not hurt. When he saw the crumpled front end of his truck, he swore loudly.

"Buddy's all right," Megan said, her head still cradled in her folded arms. Her laughter quivered with a high-pitched note of hysteria.

When she wouldn't stop, I shook her hard.

"Megan, stop it!"

She did. Wiping her wet eyes, she touched the blood on her cheek and said something unusual for Megan.

"Let's go home."

CHAPTER

THIRTEEN

Facing my parents after the car chase wasn't fun. Unfortunately, they were both downstairs when I came in, and I didn't have a chance to wash off the blood before they saw me.

"Good *lawd*!" Dad exploded. "What happened? Have you been in a fist fight?"

I shook my head. The movement made my head spin, blurring the sight of Dad's angry, anxious face.

"Did you have a wreck?" Mother's voice sounded more controlled, but her forehead was creased with worry.

"Just a little one," I muttered. "It's not as bad as it looks, honest."

"Little? You want a few broken bones thrown in?" Dad sputtered.

Mother shook her head. "Come up to the bathroom," she told me. "Let me look at your face."

While she examined the bruises on the side of my head and doctored my cut lip, she asked about Megan.

"She's okay, more or less," I said.

Megan had a cut on her face and larger bruises than I had, and though she had no one to scold her, she also had no one to care that she was hurt. While Mother wiped my face with witch hazel, I ached a little for Megan.

Dad stood in the bathroom doorway, watching Mother clean my bloody lip.

"I suppose you know that you're grounded for the rest of the weekend, young lady," he said, his voice still gruff.

"And you will *not* ride with Megan," Mother added.

"How long?"

"Until further notice," Mother said, her tone very firm.

Later, lying on my bed while my lip

168

stung and my stomach still quivered from the memory of that bone-jarring ride, I wavered between relief that the punishment wasn't worse, and a slightly disloyal feeling that I actually wouldn't mind not riding with Megan. For however long.

I took the bus to school on Monday morning. I looked for Megan when I got there, but didn't see any sign of her. It was too late to meet Kit at our usual place. Just as well; I dreaded our first meeting. He hadn't called over the weekend, and I wasn't eager to explain my injuries.

I didn't try to shadow Megan that day. I was too tired, and somehow I had the feeling that it was too late now, anyway.

In government class Susan stared at my discolored face and shook her head. "I heard you and Megan played chicken with Buddy and a freight train," she said. "You're crazy, Lacey."

"I know," I agreed.

During English class Megan seemed distracted and vague. She looked worse than I did, yellow and purple bruises across her face and a long cut down one cheek where she'd hit the rearview mirror.

"Are you all right?" I whispered during a lull in class.

"Sure, why not?" She didn't quite meet my gaze. Dark shadows that even the accident didn't explain showed under her eyes. And beneath the surface lethargy, I caught a hint of seething emotions ready to erupt —the volcano I had sensed inside her earlier.

"Megan, don't do anything stupid," I begged. "Not this week. We need a rest."

In spite of her pain she smiled the mysterious half smile that drove the boys wild.

When the lunch bell rang, I walked slowly toward the cafeteria and Kit.

He stood in the doorway and took one hard look at me. "Outside."

I followed him.

We walked into the sunlight and sat on the wall in front of the school. The anger in his eyes made me flinch.

"Have you looked in the mirror?"

"It's not as bad as it looks," I said, very low.

"I saw Buddy's truck this morning."

I nodded. "I heard his father is so mad he refused to pay for the repairs, and Buddy is furious."

170

"I don't care about Buddy's truck," Kit said. "It could have been *you*, Lacey, you and Megan who smashed into that tree. You might not have been as lucky as that idiot; you might not have walked away. How do you think I would have felt?"

In spite of my guilt, I felt a small pleasure that Kit cared whether I was hurt or not. "But we're all right."

"This time!" Kit said. "What about next time, Lacey?"

I stared at his sneakers, unable to think of an answer.

"I *told* you Megan was going to get you hurt," Kit said.

"I'm not—"

"If you could see your face!"

"Kit, I'm really sorry. It's just that Megan—"

"It's always Megan! Forget Megan. I'm worried about *you*, Lacey. You've got to promise me you'll stay out of her wild stunts."

I felt like a rubber band being pulled in two directions at once. I wanted to promise Kit anything. Yet the thought of Megan all alone—

"Please, Kit. Try to understand."

He shook his head, his face clouded with anger and frustration. "Promise me you'll stay away from her."

The band pulled tighter. I couldn't breathe. How do you choose between the two people you love most in the world?

"No," I said. "I can't."

I didn't want to see his face. I turned back toward the door.

He grabbed my shoulder, got a handful of my sweater, and something else.

The chain pulled tight around my neck, then snapped.

Kit held the remnant of the gold chain, the locket dangling from it. As he stared at the damage he'd done, the confusion inside me congealed into a cold rage.

"You can't tell me what to do, Kit. This is my decision—mine! Megan's all alone; I'm the only one she's got. What kind of a person would I be if I walked away from her? That's what love is, being there in the bad times. You can't love somebody without risking hurt. She needs me, and you don't."

I had to take a deep breath. And then I went on. "Love is dangerous, you said. Too complicated. It's your loss, Kit. Because

I'm a person worth loving. Maybe you'd better keep the locket."

Anger is a wonderful thing. It got me back inside the school, kept my head erect and my stride reasonably steady until I was out of his sight. Then I ran for the nearest rest room.

I pushed past all the curious eyes and locked myself into a stall. I leaned against the wall and let the tears roll down my cheeks, unable to sob, biting my lip against any betraying sound.

When the bell rang for the next class, I heard the shuffle of feet outside my stall. The gossip and the jokes trailed off. I made out the hiss of cigarettes snubbed out quickly in the sink, then the bang of the door as the room emptied.

When I heard nothing more, I unlocked the stall door and peeked out. No one in sight, just a haze of blue smoke from illicit cigarettes still floating in the air.

I splashed my face with cold water. The towel dispenser was empty, so I dried my cheeks with a tissue and dug through my purse for my lipstick and comb.

Nothing would hide my swollen eyelids, my red nose. I could go to class and add more fuel to the rumors racing around the school, or do the unthinkable—cut my next class.

As if in answer, the second bell rang. I was already late. Oh, who cared? I sat down in the one rickety metal folding chair, making it creak. I sat there a long time, resting my cheek against the cool gritty wall.

Sometimes, when the whole world has gone dark, you're forced to take a new look at yourself. That's what I did, sitting on that rickety metal folding chair.

Kit and I were through. I loved him so much that the ache of his absence echoed through my whole body. But love is a choice made by two people. I wouldn't run after him.

And Megan—Megan was on a suicide course, and sooner or later she'd run too far ahead of me, and I'd have to let her go. Even friendship can only stretch so far.

My parents loved me, but I would soon leave home for college. I'd leave them behind, too.

Then there would be just me—Lacey Elizabeth Walker, almost eighteen, almost adult.

I sat on the unsteady chair, in the silent smoky rest room, and looked further inside myself, afraid now of what I would see.

Take away the good student, the obedient daughter, the loyal friend and girlfriend —what else was left?

I looked back over the last few days and weeks, at the dumb and the smart things I'd done. And gradually the tension in my shoulders eased, and the knot in my stomach relaxed, and even the aching loss of Kit didn't seem as overpowering.

Even if I sometimes went about it in the wrong way, I was a person who cared about people, and that was okay, as long as I cared about myself, too. I realized that maybe it was time I started looking out for Lacey.

The shrill sound of the bell outside was followed by the shuffle of feet in the hall. Time for the next class. Time to stop hiding and face the world again. I took one more look in the mirror, then headed for the door.

The rest of the afternoon passed in a daze. Just as well that nobody else was in the mood to work, either. The students talked nonstop about the upcoming game. Even the teachers seemed to share the excitement.

Tuesday night the basketball team would travel to the district tournament. We had made it after all, and hopes for a big win were high. The pep club had plastered posters all along the wall. "Go, Rockford, go!"

In trig class the teacher, an ardent basketball fan, gave up any pretense of conducting class and let everyone discuss our chances.

"With John Paul back, we're a cinch to win," one of the boys said.

"I heard that the college scouts will be there," another boy added. "John Paul's sure to get a scholarship."

"What's his average baskets per game for the season?"

In a minute two students were working it out on the blackboard.

We had a special pep rally at two. Most of the week would probably be devoted to pep rallies and—if we were lucky—victory celebrations. I walked slowly to the gym, hoping not to see Kit, and yet depressed by the thought that he would probably avoid me if I did see him.

He didn't even come. Skipping a pep rally was an infraction of the rules, but I could guess just how much Kit cared about that right now.

I sat down on the end of the bleachers and let the cheering, the loud songs and shouts, wash over me. The school's elation seemed far away; I sat in my own circle of gloom.

I hardly noticed when Megan slipped in about the middle of the hour and sat down beside me. When the basketball players ran out onto the floor for their introduction, Megan clapped wildly.

"Don't strain yourself," I murmured.

She wasn't listening. Beneath the multicolored bruises, the cut that should have been stitched and now would probably leave a permanent scar, her face lit up with excitement.

The cheerleaders began to chant, "John Paul! John Paul!" and the crowd in the stands took it up. John Paul looked embarrassed, but Megan was ecstatic, shouting so hard I thought she would lose her voice.

Finally the coach waved the crowd into

silence and made a short speech. When he finished, the team began to walk off the court. They passed just in front of us, and Megan jumped up, waving. Then she grabbed John Paul's arm in a sort of impulsive hug.

John Paul blinked in surprise. The boy next to him frowned at Megan, and the students on the front row of the bleachers stopped cheering. I heard a few mutters and tried not to let myself distinguish the words.

John Paul looked down at Megan's blond head, gently pulled his arm from her grasp and stepped back. The worried frown, the tense lines around his deep-set dark eyes, revealed his awareness that half the school watched them.

Why couldn't John Paul just give Megan one hard putdown?

Suddenly I thought I knew.

He understood rejection.

So he was gentle with her, and no one understood. Not Megan, looking after him as the team walked off the court, her expression wistful, still hoping. Not the students who muttered among themselves, mouthing words too ugly to repeat. Certainly not Buddy, standing at the top of the bleachers, his face twisted with emotions almost beyond control.

I shivered. I wanted to grab Megan and shake some sense into her. She stood alone on the side of the court as the boys left. When the principal dismissed the crowd of students, she continued to stand there silently, while waves of kids walked around her. Not one person spoke or gave her a friendly glance.

She didn't seem to notice.

I saw Jenny on the sidelines, her pretty brown face marred by a frown as she gathered her pom-poms. I threw her a beseeching glance, hoping for support. But she ignored my unspoken plea.

"John Paul deserves better," she muttered, turning her back on us to follow the other cheerleaders off the court.

I hurried over to Megan. "I don't know what you think you're doing, but you've got to stop, *now.*"

"What are you talking about?"

"John Paul, that's what. You're not going to have a friend left at school."

"Who said I had any now?"

"I saw the way everyone looked at you.

Really, Megan, you've gone too far this time. Rockford isn't *ready* for this."

"I don't care." She smiled, her expression dreamy, and headed for the exit. "I'm going to ask him to the Valentine's dance."

"He won't go!" I ran after her through the double doors.

"We'll see."

Megan's red convertible sat on the far end of the lot. Several boys were bent over the car, and I thought I recognized one.

When Megan exclaimed, I dropped my gaze from the boys to the car. The rear tire lay flat against the pavement.

Megan swore like a sailor.

Buddy, with two of his friends, stood and grinned.

"What's the matter, Megan?" Buddy sneered. "Must be the friends you're running around with. Bad company leads to bad luck, you know."

"Buddy, you rat—" Megan raged.

"Tough luck, kid." He turned away, and the other boys, grinning, followed.

"Now what?" I murmured.

"Todd," Megan called to a boy several yards away, but he didn't seem to hear. Megan looked surprised.

I bent over and inspected the tire more closely. "It's been slashed, Megan. Ruined."

Megan waved at a couple of boys walking across the end of the parking lot. "Johnny, I need some help." The two boys gave her scornful looks and turned the other way.

We had to change the tire ourselves. The tire lugs were almost impossible to loosen, and at one point I thought it was hopeless. But when I wiped the grease off my hands, ready to give up, Megan took the wrench and tried again. She strained until her face reddened with effort. Finally we got the flat tire off and the spare on.

Neither of us spoke as we drove home. What would my parents say? Megan's expression was curiously blank.

By the time we reached my house, I was too worried about my parents' reaction to have any anxiety left for Megan. I slipped out of the car at the end of the driveway and muttered, "Talk to you later."

I walked into the house, holding my breath for an explosion. But Mother hadn't even noticed that I had come home with

Megan. She stood at the kitchen counter, slicing tomatoes.

"How was school?" she asked, her tone absentminded.

"Uh, okay."

Dad's car pulled into the drive. Mother turned her head, her expression grim, then continued to slice the vegetables.

I went to the cabinet to get out the place mats. When Dad came through the doorway, he held a bunch of flowers and a small white box. I glanced quickly at Mother, and the hard look on her face frightened me.

Don't do it, Dad, I thought. *Not again.* I remembered the first time, the time she told me about, when they were just married and she gave up the car-repair course because of him, because it wasn't "suitable" for a wife. *It won't work anymore.*

I held my breath.

Unsmiling, Mother accepted the box and lifted the lid. Her face changed; I thought she was going to cry. But her eyes lit up for the first time in weeks.

Dad put his arms around her, the forgotten flowers crushed against her back. "Sue, I'm sorry."

Her reply was muffled, but it seemed to please them both; they were kissing now. What on earth was in the little box?

"I need to turn down the stew," Mother said. Dad released her and dropped the flowers into the sink.

"Lacey," Mother said.

I jumped; I thought they'd forgotten I was there.

"Why don't you set the table? I'm going upstairs to talk to your father."

"Sure."

They went off toward the stairs, hand in hand, and I realized that Mother had left the white box sitting on the counter.

I jumped for it, dying to see what had produced such an incredible reaction. The Hope diamond, maybe?

Something even better. Inside the small box, cradled in white cotton, lay a shiny new wrench.

Who would have thought it? I remembered the long-ago auto-repair course and laughed out loud. My dad had come into the twentieth century. Kicking and screaming, maybe, but he had arrived.

I wished I could tell Kit, and then I remembered that Kit was no longer part of my life. The memory brought back the pain, deep inside. Pushing the ache away, I headed for the door. I could talk to Megan.

I walked across the road, going as usual toward the back door. But the driveway was empty, the red convertible missing.

My heart beat fast. Where had she gone? There was no one in this whole town except me who would want to see Megan tonight.

But there was one person *she* wanted to see. I had to find her. Who knew what else Buddy might do?

Running back home, I pushed open the kitchen door and grabbed the phone.

Surely Kit wouldn't let me down if I needed him.

I tried his home number first. The phone rang, but no one answered. I slammed down the receiver in frustration, then picked it up and punched the buttons again, this time for the drugstore.

"May I speak to Kit, please?"

"He's not here, Lacey," Mr. Patton told me. "He's driving his mother to Biloxi."

"Oh."

I heard the druggist say, "Lacey, is something wrong?"

"I need him," I said, too worried to care how crazy I sounded. "I need him."

I hung up the phone, trying to think. Then I saw Dad's car keys, where he had left them on the counter.

I hesitated only a moment. Then I scribbled a note for my parents, grabbed the keys, and ran for the car.

CHAPTER

FOURTEEN

The drive to John Paul's house seemed to take forever. All the way I prayed, without words, but for what I wasn't sure. I hoped I would find Megan there, and hoped against hope that she'd had too much sense to go near the place.

I had a hard time locating the address. Even when I found the lane, I couldn't remember which was the right house. When I saw a small pigtailed girl playing alongside the mailbox, my heart leapt. I stopped the car and got out, hoping not to frighten her.

"Aren't you John Paul's sister?"

Her brown eyes widened.

"Did Megan—did a blond-haired girl come here looking for John Paul?"

She pulled her thumb out of her mouth and said, "The one in the nice red car?"

"Yes! Did she speak to John Paul?"

The little girl shook her head, then volunteered, "He's at work." The child thought a moment, then added, "I told her, too."

"Where does he work?"

"At the gas station."

"Where is it?"

The thumb slipped back into her mouth, and she stared at me blankly.

I sighed.

An older girl looked out the front door and stared at me. "Lana, come here!"

Lana ran for the house. I hurried back to my car.

"What's the use?" I asked myself. "Stay out of it."

But Megan was out there, somewhere, and I was afraid of what she might do. I *couldn't* stay out of it. I had to find her.

It was getting dark now, and all the streets in this part of town looked alike. I drove in circles for long minutes until common sense told me that Rockford didn't have that many service stations. I finally discovered the red convertible at a run-down gas station on the south side of town.

I pulled in next to the curb, a few feet down the street. Megan stood in front of the gas pumps, talking quickly and passionately to John Paul. John Paul shook his head. Megan reached out to grab his arm, as if she could force him to listen.

Then I heard the growl of a powerful engine. Buddy and two of his friends roared up in the yellow pickup with the crumpled front end. The truck skidded into the station, and the boys piled out.

My heart began to beat like a military drum, fast and hard. There were few buildings on this stretch of side street, only a vacant lot and several small stores, deserted now that the sunset faded behind the store fronts. Down the street a small beer joint flashed a red neon light, but the thought of entering that gloomy-looking shack made my pulse jump even faster.

The boys advanced on Megan and John Paul, who seemed still absorbed in their argument. I opened the car door as quietly as possible. My knees were weak, but I had to do something.

I took two steps toward the tavern, dreading the thought of trying to explain. Would they let me in the door, being underage? Megan might have bluffed her way through, but not me.

I glanced anxiously back at Megan and saw that Buddy and his gang stood just in front of her. John Paul had turned to face the newcomers. Megan shouted at Buddy, but he paid her as little notice as he would pay a whining mosquito. It was John Paul the boys watched, John Paul who stood tense, his fists clenched, his dark face hard and still in comprehension of his danger.

I couldn't move. Buddy swung an almost casual blow toward the black ball player. John Paul stepped forward and threw up one arm to block it. The other two boys lunged, then they were holding John Paul, despite his struggles, one on each side. Buddy hit the ball player hard in the stomach.

Megan screamed.

I remembered the championship game tomorrow night, and the college scouts who were coming to watch John Paul play. If he didn't play, would he lose his chance for a scholarship—his ticket out of Rockford, away from poverty and frustration?

Megan, I thought, *what have you done?*

I started toward them, but something grabbed me from behind.

I shrieked.

It was Kit.

I sobbed from sheer relief and leaned against him.

"What is it, Lacey?"

"I thought you were gone."

"I left my jacket at the drugstore. When I stopped to pick it up, Mr. Patton told me about your call. I had to find out what was wrong. When I went by your house, I found the note you left. I figured things out from there."

"Kit, look," I gestured toward the fight. "We've got to stop them."

For the first time he looked beyond me to the scene under the tall lights, and we both heard the muffled impact of fist against flesh. Kit's face tightened.

"I'll go to the tavern," I said.

Kit shook his head. "Try the gas station; it should have a phone. Call the sheriff."

"Be careful," I begged as he started for the boys. Not daring to look again, I ran across the oil-stained pavement toward the station.

Inside the doorway I glanced frantically around the cluttered office. When I saw the telephone, I almost fell over a chair as I jumped for it. But the cord was frayed, and when I held the receiver to my ear, the line was dead.

I heard angry voices beyond the door. I had no time, no time. Then, on the wall beyond the phone, I saw a box outlined in red, with a fire extinguisher and a button that said, *In case of fire.*

I grabbed a rusty spanner off the pile of junk on the desk and shattered the glass over the case. I pushed the button, hard, and waited for the wail of an alarm.

Nothing happened.

Now what? Run to the tavern and hope someone would listen? The thought of silent men hunched over mugs of beer offered little reassurance. I wasn't even sure which side they would choose to champion. Hesitating, I turned back toward the front of the station.

John Paul still struggled in the grip of

Buddy's pals, blood dripping from his face. Kit stood between John Paul and Buddy. Buddy gestured angrily.

Kit seemed small and slight in comparison to Buddy—Kit, who had stepped into an impossible fight, who had answered my call for help, because he loved me, because he knew what was right.

Buddy swung. Kit swayed from the impact, then straightened and lashed back.

Megan put her hands to her face. She had stopped screaming; she looked dazed and sick.

Buddy staggered under Kit's blow, but when he fell against the gas pump, he came back up with a heavy pipe in his hand.

I tried to scream, but there was no sound, only the brutal clarity of the pipe falling, hitting Kit's arm as he threw it up to protect himself. The bone snapped; Kit slumped forward. I started to run.

I threw myself at Buddy, dimly aware that he raised his arm again. I saw the rage in his eyes and his lips drawn back over his teeth like a mad dog. Then the world exploded, and there was only darkness.

CHAPTER

FIFTEEN

A sledgehammer pounded against the back of my head. Why didn't someone make it stop?

I struggled to open my eyes, making out a window shaded by cream-colored blinds. It was not my window. I looked down at the bed, narrow and hard, and it was not my bed. I forgot the pounding for a moment. What was I was doing here?

My mother sat on a straight chair beside the bed. Dark circles showed under her eyes; she looked very tired. I wanted to ask her what was wrong, but my mouth seemed to be full of cotton wool.

Mother raised her head. When she saw my half-opened eyes, she smiled, and the lines of tension in her face softened.

If Mother smiled at me, it must be all right.

I tried to move my head, but it seemed too heavy, and the effort only made the pounding worse. My mouth ached with dryness. Mother leaned forward and offered me a glass with a bent straw so that I could take a sip.

The tepid water eased my arid mouth, but I still couldn't talk. My mind seemed as full of cotton as my mouth had been.

Mother stroked my forehead softly. I forgot the questions I wanted to ask, and my eyes closed again.

When I woke the next time, daylight filled the room, though dimly, past closed shades. Mother sat in the same chair, her head slightly forward, dozing. I watched her for a minute; she looked so tired and pale that through all my confusion I felt a rush of guilt.

How had I ended up here?

I tried to move my head. The pain was still there, though duller, and movement didn't exactly help. I gasped, and the slight sound was enough to wake Mother. She stood up quickly.

"Lacey? How do you feel?"

"Not too bad," I lied.

My words sounded garbled, even to me, but she understood.

"Good."

She picked up the glass of water and held it so that I could take a sip.

"What happened?" I said.

"You were hit on the head, honey. You've had a concussion."

I tried to sort out my memories; it was like looking at a video that's been badly edited, all choppy and confused.

"Is Kit all right? And John Paul and Megan?" My voice squeaked with anxiety.

Mother nodded. "They're all—more or less—in good shape."

"Will John Paul be able to play tomorrow night?" As more came back to me, more worries flooded my mind.

"He was brilliant, Lacey. Kit says his scholarship is a sure thing. He's already talking to two colleges."

197

What did she mean *was*? I blinked in bewilderment.

Mother pushed a strand of hair from my cheek. "You've been unconscious for three days, Lacey."

Oh, boy. The dark circles under my mother's eyes, the lines etched in her forehead—I felt another stab of guilt. What must she have been thinking? All those babies she had lost, all those little graves. How could I have put her through this?

"I'm sorry," I whispered. "Rushing out like that, it was just—" How could I explain?

"I know," she said simply. Mother understood about love.

I lay back against the sheets, some of my tension fading.

"Someone has been waiting very patiently to see you. The doctor hasn't approved visitors, yet, but I suppose we could allow him five minutes."

My face must have lit up. She patted my hand gently and went out the door.

Kit came in very quietly, his face drawn with lines of worry and almost fearful anticipation. I felt an absurd desire to cry. Trying to control the tears, it was a moment before I saw that his left arm was in a sling. Staring at the white cast, I said, "Oh, Kit!"

"I'm fine," he assured me, sitting down. "You're the one who had everyone worried."

"I didn't know—three days. What happened, Kit?"

"When you collapsed, I jumped on Buddy again, and John Paul went crazy. He broke the collarbone of one of the goons holding him. Then the fire truck arrived."

"Fire truck?"

"You set off an alarm inside the station, Lacey. Don't you remember?"

"But there was no bell; I thought it didn't work."

"It had a line to the fire station," Kit explained. "They were pretty surprised to see a fight instead of a fire, but they pulled everybody apart and called the sheriff."

"And?"

"John Paul's okay. We won the game by fifteen points, so he's a big hero again, and his college plans are solid. I think," Kit grinned slightly, "he won that game for you, Lacey."

I felt my cheeks flush. "I'm glad he's okay," I said. "What about Buddy?"

"He and his gang are out on bail, but they're saying Buddy may have to stand trial as an adult; he'll be eighteen next month."

"And Megan?"

Kit looked away for a moment. What had happened to Megan?

"She'll tell you; she's spent almost as much time sitting in the corridor as I have. The nurses would only allow one person in your room, and your mother wouldn't listen to any arguments, so your dad and I have spent the last few evenings playing gin rummy. He owes me three dollars and ten cents."

I tried to laugh, but all that came out was a squeak.

Kit took my hand and held it tightly. He glanced at his watch. "Before they run me out, I have something to give you." He gave my hand one last squeeze, then reached inside his shirt pocket. He drew out a small box and opened it awkwardly with his good hand.

I felt tears swell behind my lids when I recognized the locket. I blinked hard.

He flipped it open. Inside it still said, "To Lacey, from Kit," but on the front one word had been added—"Love."

My throat closed up. The locket had a new, heavier chain. Kit held it out hesitantly.

"Do you still want it?"

I didn't trust my voice, so I nodded, despite the ache in my head, and Kit placed the locket in my hand.

"You're still going off to college next fall, without any strings," Kit said, his voice firm. Then he added, "But complications or not, I love you, Lacey."

"I'm glad," I told him. "I love you, too."

He leaned over the bed and kissed me gently, smoothing away a stray tear on my cheek with his good hand.

"I'd better go," he said. "Just get well, okay?"

After he left, my dad came in to give me a hug, then the nurse shooed everyone out and took my blood pressure. I had so much to think about that I knew I wouldn't rest. So I was more surprised than the nurse must have been when I drifted back to sleep before she even got the arm band off.

They woke me when the doctor came,

then Mother helped me eat a bowl of watery broth. Afterwards she said, "You have someone else waiting to see you."

I nodded, expecting Megan. But it was John Paul who came in. He looked very tall, standing in the doorway.

He hesitated, then walked closer to the bed and gave me a quick, shy smile. His cheekbones were broad and strong, his eyes clear and bright. He looked intelligent and vibrant and very much alive, as if energy and good health were currents coursing through his whole, clean-limbed body.

I suddenly saw just how attractive he was. For the first time I saw him as a person, not a black boy in a white town. No wonder Megan had been attracted to him. He had been kind to her, and she had known little kindness in her life. Awkward passion she had had, but not kindness.

John Paul's voice was deep and husky. "I wanted to thank you, Lacey."

Not expecting that, I flushed. He had dropped the protective mask of polite reserve. All those hours we had spent in the same classroom, and I'd never had a glimpse of the real person before. I felt

humbled and childish, for having been
blind to so much.

"I didn't really—"

"Yes, you did," he contradicted gently.
"I thanked Kit, too, but Kit came because
of you."

But I was there because of Megan, I
thought, feeling guilty for thanks I didn't
deserve. I was afraid to mention Megan.

"I'm glad you won the game," I told
him.

He grinned. "The team won the game."

"But you got your scholarship?"

John Paul nodded. I saw the bright fires
inside his eyes that revealed how close he
had come to losing his dream.

"That's the only thing that matters," I
told him.

John Paul shook his head. "What matters," he said, "is that when I remember
Buddy, and—some other people in this
town—I can remember decent people, too.
It helps."

He stood up and seemed ready to leave.
Something was missing, but I wasn't sure
what.

He was quicker than I was. He grinned
the quiet, slight curve of the lips that he

had never revealed in his public face, and held out his hand.

I took it; he had a firm grip.

"Good luck, John Paul," I told him, knowing that he wasn't going to need luck anymore.

When he left, I lay quietly, thinking. Mother came to check on me, and I looked at her expectantly.

"Do you feel up to another visitor?"

I nodded.

And, at last, there was Megan.

"I wasn't sure you'd want to see me," she said. Her voice sounded gruff, but I could hear the pain.

I held out my arms to her, and she hugged me, as if we were little again, clinging together when the noises in the dark became too menacing. Only this time the fears were real, and the pain had not been imagined.

"Lacey, I'm sorry."

I hugged her again. For a moment she let me hold her, then pulled back and wiped away the dampness on her lashes.

I blinked. Megan was crying.

"I didn't mean it to happen like that," she said.

"I know."

She sat on the edge of the bed. "I thought—I told myself that I really cared about him, Lacey. For the first time in my life, I believed I might really be in love. I was so caught up in how *I* felt, I didn't think about *his* feelings. I was so sure I didn't care what the town did to me—" Her voice faltered.

"You wanted to shock them," I pointed out mildly. "As usual."

She nodded. "But I didn't consider what they might do to *him*. I'm not very good at thinking about other people, Lacey, not like you."

Until you do, you won't know what love is, I thought, but I couldn't bring myself to say it.

She went on. "Know what John Paul said to me, that night at the station, before Buddy came?"

"What?"

"He said, 'You have no right to do this to me.' And I said, 'But, John Paul, I love you.' "

I waited.

"And he said"—her voice broke, and she took a deep breath to steady it—" 'But *I* don't love *you*, Megan.' He said it very nicely, Lacey, but he said it."

"You can't make a person love you, Megan," I told her. "Not John Paul, not your father. But if you can learn to like yourself, someone else can learn to love you."

"Your mother said something like that," Megan murmured. "I didn't mean to hurt John Paul—or you, Lacey. I never meant to hurt you. When I saw you fall—I wished it were me."

I reached out to touch her arm. "I'm fine, Megan, honest. I talked to the doctor before dinner. They may let me go home tomorrow."

She let me clasp her hand for a moment —Megan, who hated to be touched. She looked as drawn and haggard as my mother had when I'd first come around. Megan was too young to look so defeated.

"Megan, there's something else, isn't there? Has your dad come home? What'd he say?"

I could barely hear her words. "Somebody told him I was chasing after—we had a big fight. He threw me out. He said I was just as bad as my mother. I guess I always wondered."

"Are you serious?"

"I've been staying at your house. I had a long talk with your mother. She said I should call my aunt in Ohio and talk to her, so I did."

I couldn't believe it. "And?"

Megan shrugged. "She sounds—okay, I guess. She wants me to come stay with her for a while."

"But, Megan, we graduate in four months!"

Megan looked directly at me. "I don't have enough credits to graduate with the class, Lacey. The guidance counselor told me two weeks ago. You always warned me about my grades, remember?"

I remembered. But I still felt shocked. Megan had always talked herself out of trouble. I couldn't believe that this time it was all coming home.

"What will you do? Start in a new high school?"

"I don't think so. Maybe take the GED and go to business school. Maybe look for a job. I'll see. But I think I've had enough of Rockford. And I think Rockford's had enough of me." She laughed, but the sound held a bitter note.

"Megan," I said. "It's never too late. You'll do better, next time. I know you will."

"That's what your mother said." Megan's hands were clenched tightly in her lap. "You're a lot like your mother, Lacey. You're lucky. I used to envy you so much—wish I could be like you."

"You did?" I was too astonished to appreciate the irony of this revelation.

This time she reached out to me of her own volition, and we hugged again. I thought how I would miss her.

I tried to tell her. She only grinned, the old grin with the quirk in it, and shook her head. "You'll be busy at college in a few months, with Kit and lots of new friends."

"I won't forget you, Megan." I tried to keep my voice steady. "I never fell off the roof for anyone else. Maybe next winter vacation I'll come up to visit you and see the snow. You always said I should travel."

For some reason this struck us both as witty, and we laughed wildly. When Megan stood up, some of the pain in her face had eased.

"Thanks, Lacey."

"For what?"

"Looking out for me. Caring."

She walked quickly out the door. I closed my eyes for a minute, remembering. When the memories became too much, I opened my eyes and looked toward the doorway.

And Kit stood there silently, waiting.

Dear Reader:

Looking Out for Lacey is about love and friendship, surely two of the most powerful forces in anyone's life. When the two conflict, as they do for Lacey, it's not an easy choice—not when it's a genuine love, a deep and long-lasting friendship.

I know about small towns, where everyone knows your life story, and the South, where I spent a good part of my childhood. Born in Tennessee, I was an Army brat and have also lived in Georgia, Mississippi, Germany, Scotland, and California. Now I've come full circle, back to Tennessee.

I've loved books since the day I was introduced to Mother Goose, and I've wanted to write almost as long. After college and several years of teaching, I took a year off to write full time and sold my first novel after thirteen months. Over twenty books later, I've discovered that writing has its ups and downs, but I wouldn't trade this crazy career for any other.

I also enjoy old movies, plays, traveling, dogs, cats, horses, and good friends, and love is the whipped cream on the sundae. Writing is still my passion, and reading my joy.

Cheryl Zach

Read the next dramatic Changes
romance, coming in May.

THE
UNBELIEVABLE
TRUTH

CHAPTER

ONE

Everyone said Hannah looked great, for a dead person.

Don't ask me. I couldn't bring myself to look.

Still, as funerals go, it was a big success. Lots of wailing and sobbing and carrying on. Hannah would've loved it. She was a real weeper: soaps, *Lassie* reruns, you name it. I once saw her cry over a dead philodendron.

Me, I didn't shed a tear, not even when the school choir sang "Amazing Grace" a cappella, and the whole audience got into some serious nose-blowing. Who were they to cry? I was her best friend.

Of course, everyone was Hannah's friend. Hannah was the 7-Eleven of pals: open twenty-four hours, catering to every need. She was a fixer. A rescuer. It didn't much matter what: sick plants, stray animals, prison parolees. Hannah loved a challenge.

I was fifteen when Hannah adopted me. Sure, I already had a mother. But Hannah had this stubborn maternal streak that wrapped around you like a thick quilt on a summer morning—you really didn't need it, but you couldn't quite bring yourself to shake it off, either.

"You're all alone." That's what she'd said by way of introduction, hovering over me in the lunchroom the day we met. Reeking of Charlie, as I recall. Day one of our sophomore year. Black Monday, I'd christened it. It would be over a hundred more Mondays till I could graduate and hightail it out of there.

You're all alone.

I blinked, took a swig of cola, considered. "You have a stunning grasp of the obvious," I said. I was brand-new to Maine and still sulking splendidly. I hated every damp, gray, square inch of the place.

Hannah stood undaunted, lunch tray poised, waiting for the invitation I had no intention of issuing. "I think you need a friend," she said matter-of-factly, and she promptly sat down and proceeded to become one.

I couldn't believe her nerve. But that was Hannah, all over. She'd known I was alone, and that was all it took. She figured all of us were alone, one way or another, and she passed out emotional Band-Aids to everyone she knew.

But as it turned out, no one knew Hannah, not even Matt, not even me. Least of all me.

No doubt she loved the irony. Hannah was big on irony. Who'd have guessed it of prudent, sensible Hannah Ward? The girl who used seat belts and sunscreen with religious fervor.

Who'd have guessed there was another Hannah? The Hannah who swallowed a couple handfuls of tiny blue pills and drifted off for good.

Hannah, all alone.

I listened to the minister and the principal and the parade of snifflers, talking about how Hannah had touched their lives, and all I could think was, Why didn't we see it? Where were the clues? What did we do wrong?

What did *I* do wrong?

Some friend. You couldn't say I killed Hannah, exactly, but I didn't stop her from dying, either.

We sat there stiffly, Matt and Dr. Ward and I, eyes unblinking, hot and dry as coals. The three of us, praying for the luxury of tears. Waiting for Hannah to rain down forgiveness. What fools.

Before the funeral, they asked me if I wanted to say anything. Matt volunteered instead. He read a poem Hannah's mom had written years ago, Hannah's favorite. But what could I have said? Hannah's gone, guys, and the rest of us are stuck here to clean up her mess. Each of us, all alone.